[Photo credit] © Michael Lamb 2010

KU-525-218

STACY GREGG grew up training her bewildered dog to showjump in the backyard until her parents gave in to her desperate pleas and finally let her have a pony. Stacy's ponies and her experiences at her local pony club were the inspiration for the *Pony Club Secrets* books, and her later years at boarding school became the catalyst for the *Pony Club Rivals* series.

Pictured here with her beloved Dutch Warmblood gelding, Ash, Stacy is a board member of the Horse Welfare Auxiliary.

Find out more at: www.stacygregg.co.uk

Windsor and Maidenhead

38067100544731

The Pony Club Rivals series:

1. *The Auditions*

Coming soon...

2. *Showjumpers*

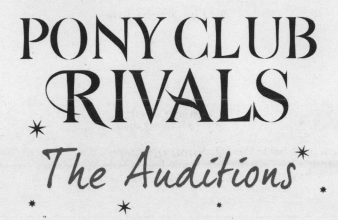

PONY CLUB RIVALS
The Auditions

STACY GREGG

HarperCollins *Children's Books*

www.stacygregg.co.uk

First published in Great Britain by HarperCollins *Children's Books* in 2010
HarperCollins *Children's Books* is a division of HarperCollins*Publishers* Ltd,
77-85 Fulham Palace Road, Hammersmith, London, W6 8JB

2

Text copyright © Stacy Gregg 2010

ISBN 978-0-00-733343-1

Stacy Gregg asserts the moral right to be identified
as the author of the work.

Printed and bound in England by Clays Ltd, St Ives plc

Chapter One

The black gelding snorted and fretted, moving anxiously from side to side in the start box. Holding him back, the girl tightened her grip on the reins as she waited for the steward to check his clipboard.

"Number forty-two... forty-two... let me see..." the steward ran his eyes down the list, "forty-two... here you are! Georgina Parker, yes?" He cast a glance at the pony dancing and crab-stepping. "And this must be Tyro."

As the steward said his name, the black pony went straight up on his hind legs in a half-rear and then lunged forward, trying to bolt. The sudden movement threw his rider back in the saddle, but she regained her seat with lightning speed. Before the pony could get

5

away, she had pulled hard to the left, turning him in a tight circle so that he was back in the same position as moments before, in the start box facing out over the hill that led down to the first jump of the cross-country course.

"Nearly lost you!" the steward joked. "You don't want to fall off before you even get started, do you?"

"Falling off is most definitely not part of the plan," Georgie agreed. She was trying to stay calm, but as the steward fussed over his clipboard she could feel the adrenalin surging through her. She was ready to go and so was Tyro. *Hurry up*, she thought, *I can't keep holding him! My arms already feel as feeble as worn-out knicker elastic from hanging on so long!*

The steward seemed to understand her silent plea. "Right then, bring him up to the start line," he told her. "Are you ready? On your marks… and… three… two… one… GO!"

Tyro broke from the start box and this time Georgie didn't try to hold him back. She stood up in her stirrups like a jockey and put her reins in her left hand, freeing up her right hand to press the button on her stopwatch.

She was battling the clock today. She had to make it round the course with a clear round and no time faults if she wanted to retain her first place ranking.

This morning in the dressage arena, Georgie and Tyro had done their best-ever test and totally aced the first phase of the one-day event. Right now, they were just ahead of Georgie's closest rival, Daisy King, at the top of the leader board. But the scores were tight. There were only two points between Georgie and Daisy, and there were several other riders hot on her heels just a few points behind. Georgie would need to bring her A-game and get a perfect round in both the cross-country and showjumping phases to maintain her lead.

From the moment that morning when horse lorries and trailers had begun arriving at the Great Brampton grounds, Georgie had sensed the tension in the air. So much was riding on this competition, not just for her, but for hundreds of young eventing riders from across the UK gathered here today. All of them had just one aim: to make it into the top three and survive this gruelling semi-final audition and progress to the grand finals in Birmingham. There, they would battle it out against riders from every discipline to become the chosen ones. In the end, only five finalists would be selected. Their prize: admission to the famed Blainford Academy in Lexington, USA.

Blainford Academy had been Georgie's dream ever since she could remember. The exclusive equestrian boarding school was *the* place to go if you were serious about becoming a professional horse rider. No other college could rival Blainford's record. It was known as the 'All-Stars Academy' since its graduates were the world champions in every kind of equestrian sport.

Blainford's recruitment process was international. The academy's talent scouts travelled the world, holding auditions for the very best riders from around the globe. Thousands of riders applied, but only a few could be chosen – and Georgie was determined that she was going to be one of them.

A win at Great Brampton would send Georgie straight through to the Birmingham grand finals in two weeks' time. As they flew out of the start box she could feel success within her grasp. The cross-country course was the biggest Georgie had ever tackled but she had faith in Tyro's abilities. The pony was fit and keen and as they approached the first jump he was galloping on strongly, his ears pricked forward with excitement, ready to face whatever lay ahead.

✳

Fence one was a low hedge, no more than half a metre high. Tyro had jumped twice this height in the paddock at home, but Georgie wasn't taking any chances. She rode at it with such fierce determination you'd have sworn she was attacking the huntsman's close at the Badminton Horse Trials.

Tyro flew the hedge and Georgie gave the gelding a slappy pat on his jet-black neck, "Good boy!" She picked up the pace again and galloped him on towards a fallen log positioned at the top of a steep bank.

Georgie had to steady Tyro as he was galloping a little too fast. Then, as he took the jump, she leaned back to keep her balance, keeping her weight over his rump as he flew the log with a big stride that took him halfway down the bank. In two quick downhill strides he was at the bottom and Georgie straightened back up

9

again. She stood up in her stirrups in two-point position and rode him hard towards the next fence already looming ahead of them; a narrow rustic gate. Tyro popped it as if it weren't even there, and Georgie leant down low and murmured words of encouragement as she pressed him to go faster. Tyro seemed to understand and extended his stride, galloping beautifully as they neared the water complex.

Of all the fences on the course it was the water complex that had Georgie worried. Tyro hadn't always been the bravest pony when it came to water jumps and so, with her heart hammering in her chest, she rode him on boldly at the brush fence that led into the water.

"Come on!" she shouted to encourage him as they approached the jump. But there was no need. Tyro leapt confidently, without hesitation into the pond. The murky brown water churned into a wake behind them as he cantered towards the low bank at the other end of the pond.

As they reached the low bank, Georgie felt the pony prepare to take off. She could feel him picking up underneath her, and then in one awful moment it all went wrong. Instead of jumping out and on to the bank, Tyro plummeted down into the water. It was as if the pony's legs had collapsed beneath him. He fell down hard, twisting and somersaulting on to his back, taking a horrified Georgie with him as he went under the water.

Georgie didn't even have time to scream as they fell. She felt the ice-cold shock of the water and then Tyro was right on top of her, pushing her under, crushing her with the enormous weight of his body.

Georgie tried to take a last gasp of air but inhaled dirty water instead. The pond was no more than a metre deep, but that was deep enough. She was submerged underneath Tyro, and the pony was flailing about on top of her trying to get back on his feet again.

Then, in a sudden rush, the massive weight of the pony was gone. Tyro had managed to stand up, and now Georgie was fighting her way up too, struggling to breathe as she broke the surface, coughing up lungfuls of scummy pond water.

The jump steward was the first person to reach her. His face was white with shock and Georgie realised that the fall must have been quite spectacular.

11

"Are you OK?" the steward asked as he waded into the water and grasped Tyro's reins, holding him while Georgie stood up. She was shaky on her feet, but she was standing and she was breathing, and since a few moments ago neither of these was possible, she was quite relieved.

"That was a really bad fall," the steward said. "Are you hurt? Do you need me to get the ambulance?"

"I'm fine," Georgie was still coughing, trying to get her breath back, "although I think I might have swallowed a tadpole..."

"Georgie!" There was a shout from the sidelines and Georgie turned round to see a woman with brown hair leap over the rope fence and run towards her.

"What happened?" the woman asked when she reached Georgie's side.

"I don't know!" Georgie shook her head. "He was about to jump. I felt him lift up and then something went wrong and he went down so fast..."

"Are you her mother?" the steward asked.

"No," the woman replied. "I'm Lucinda Milwood, I'm her trainer."

Lucinda took the reins from the steward and led Tyro up on to the bank beside the pond while Georgie hunted in the muddy, churned-up pond muck for her riding crop. She found it floating near the edge by some reeds and ran up the bank to rejoin Lucinda who was bent down over Tyro's front legs.

"I think I've figured out what happened," Lucinda said. "Look at this!"

She pulled the bell boot off Tyro's left front hoof and handed it to Georgie. There was a huge rip in the rubber.

"I think that's what did it," Lucinda said. "He must have stood on his own boot with one of his hind legs, and then when he tried to jump he tripped himself up instead! No wonder he fell so suddenly."

"Ohmygod!" Georgie shook her head in stunned disbelief.

"It was just bad luck," Lucinda said gently, "there was nothing you could have done..."

There was a commotion on the sidelines as a man emerged at the front of the crowd, jumped over the rope barrier and ran towards Georgie and Lucinda.

13

"Sorry, sir." The steward stepped forward to stop him. "Spectators aren't allowed on the track right now. There's been an accident with this young rider and we need to clear the course for the next competitor..."

"I'm a doctor," the man responded firmly. He looked at Georgie standing in sodden jodhpurs beside the bedraggled Tyro. "And I'm also her father."

"I know it looks bad, Alastair, but they're both all right..." Lucinda tried to reassure him, but Dr Parker ignored her and began to examine Georgie, peering into her eyes, checking to see if her pupils were dilated.

"Dad! Stop it! I'm totally fine!" Georgie couldn't believe her luck! Why did her dad have to be watching at this fence? Having him fuss over her like this in front of everyone when all she wanted to do was get back on Tyro was so frustrating.

Dr Parker however was oblivious to Georgie's impatience. "Were you knocked out at any point?" he asked as he continued to look into her eyes. "Do you remember everything that happened?"

"She's not hurt, Alastair," Lucinda tried to tell him but Dr Parker snapped at her.

"…and you're not a doctor, Lucinda, so please let me take care of my daughter!"

"I'm terribly sorry…" the steward interrupted, "but we really do need to clear the course now. Is she going to mount up and continue?"

"What?" Dr Parker looked shocked at the idea. "She most certainly is not!"

"Dad! I can do it!" Georgie pleaded. "Lucinda, tell him! I need to finish!"

But her trainer shook her head. "Your father is right. Let's take Tyro back to the truck."

"But we'll be eliminated!" Georgie couldn't believe Lucinda was agreeing with her dad.

"Georgie," Lucinda said gently, "you've had a fall. Elimination doesn't matter now. You could get back on and finish the course but that won't change anything… it's over."

Deep down Georgie knew that there was no point in getting back on. A fall on the cross-country course automatically cost a rider sixty faults. And this fall had cost her much more than that. With sixty faults there was no way she could win. All those hours of training

15

had been reduced to nothing in one brief moment of misfortune at the water jump. Her dream had been lost forever. She had failed the auditions for Blainford Academy.

✳

At Little Brampton Stables that evening, Georgie checked Tyro over one more time, running her hands down his legs looking for any signs of heat that might indicate an injury. The black pony seemed sound enough, so she threw on his lightweight summer rug, and turned him out in the field with his hard feed.

Georgie watched as Tyro snuffled about eagerly consuming the contents of his feed bucket. He was a greedy pony and a quick eater, and always managed to hoover up every last crumb.

With the now empty feed bucket under her arm, Georgie headed back to the tack room to deal with Tyro's saddle and bridle. They were caked in mud from the fall so she sat down on a pile of old horse rugs with a cake of saddle soap and a cloth and got to work on the stirrup leathers.

Georgie loved the tack room at Lucinda's stables. It smelt of horse sweat and leather, and sometimes a little bit of dead mouse, but she didn't mind that too much. She often sat in here and looked at the walls, covered with her trainer's rosettes, ribbons and photographs.

As she began to wipe down Tyro's bridle, Georgie's eyes scanned the walls. There were photos of Lucinda, taken at school when she was a student at Blainford. Lucinda hadn't changed much since those days and looked just the same, with her smiling eyes and her brown hair in a messy ponytail. The girl who featured in most of the photos with Lucinda also had long brown hair and a broad smile. She was Ginny Parker, Georgie's mum and Lucinda Milwood's best friend at Blainford. After they left school Ginny had gone on to become a famous international eventing rider and it was no secret that Georgie wanted to follow in her footsteps.

Georgie's favourite picture on the wall was an action shot of her mother riding a bay mare named Boudicca. They were in full flight over a massive stone wall, the mare had her ears pricked forward and Ginny's hazel eyes were focused intently on the next jump ahead.

Georgie missed her mum so much. She knew it probably wouldn't have changed the outcome if she had been there today. But she wished more than anything that her mum were here to give her a hug, to tell her that what happened on the cross-country course wasn't her fault and that everything would be OK.

Hot tears made their way down Georgie's cheeks. She reached up and brushed them away angrily with the back of her hand. There was no point in being like this, Georgie told herself. No use sniffling and feeling sorry for herself and hoping for things that weren't going to happen. She had lost at Great Brampton and nothing would change that. And it was no good wishing her mum was here. Because Ginny Parker was gone, and she wasn't coming back.

Chapter Two

Georgie's fall at Great Brampton undoubtedly delighted Daisy King, who rose up from second place in the rankings and rode brilliantly to take first place. Strangely enough however, it wasn't just Georgie's rivals who were happy that she'd lost. Her friends were chuffed as well.

"I can't help it. I think it's brilliant news!" Lily said when Georgie told her about the water jump disaster at school the following day. "Honestly, Georgie. You're my best friend and I can't stand the idea of you leaving to go to some posh, horsey school in America."

Georgie sighed. She should have known better than to expect sympathy from Lily.

"I mean," Lily continued, "I don't even understand

19

why you want to go to boarding school anyway. It's like wanting to go to prison!"

"Blainford's not just a boarding school," Georgie countered with exasperation. "It's an elite training school with horses." She didn't know why she bothered. It was the same old argument they'd had a million times. Georgie couldn't blame her best friend for being anti-Blainford. After all, if Georgie actually managed to get a place at the academy then it would mean moving away from Little Brampton and away from Lily. They had been best friends ever since they met at Little Brampton primary school at the age of four. Now they were thirteen and in their second year at Little Brampton High School.

"They feed you gruel at boarding school, you know," Lily continued.

"What's gruel?" Georgie asked.

"It's like porridge only worse; tasteless and runny," Lily told her. "I read a book about a boarding school where the children all got gruel and were whipped with a birch stick when they were naughty."

Georgie groaned, "Maybe if you went to boarding

school two hundred years ago it was like that, Lily. I don't think anyone gets beaten with a birch stick at Blainford."

"I bet they still have the gruel though," Lily was insistent.

"The worst bit about yesterday," Georgie said, changing the subject, "was after I fell off. I was walking back to the horse truck with Tyro, all soaked and grubby and everyone on the sidelines was watching us, and then my dad says really loudly so that everyone can hear, 'Never mind, Georgina, how about I buy you an ice cream on the way home to cheer you up!'" Georgie rolled her eyes. "As if I was a four-year-old who'd lost a lollipop – not an eventing rider who'd just taken a fall on the cross-country course!"

Lily giggled. "Your dad just doesn't get it, does he?"

Georgie shook her head. "He doesn't understand me, full stop. He never has really."

"He's no worse than my dad," Lily said. "He doesn't have a clue about me either. At least your dad was willing to let you apply to Blainford, even though the school fees must cost a bomb."

"It's not like it was Dad's idea. He hates the thought of me going there. Mum was the one who had my name down on the enrolment list from the day I was born."

It had been a massive battle for Georgie to convince Dr Parker to let her apply for Blainford. Her dad didn't understand why she wanted to go. "You already have a pony," he told her. "Why can't you stay here and save riding for after school and the weekends? The local high school is perfectly adequate."

"No, it's not," Georgie had told him. "Not if I want to become a world-class rider. All the best riders in the world have been to Blainford. You get to take your horse with you and you can ride every day, plus there are specialist riding classes and they teach all sorts of horse subjects as well as the regular stuff like English and maths."

"I think you're being swayed by the fact that your mother went to school there," Dr Parker said. "I'm sure if we look around we could find an equestrian school here in Gloucestershire that is just as good. I believe there are several excellent ones in the county. Why does it have to be this Blainford – on the other side of the world in America?"

"Blainford is the best," Georgie countered. "It's not just because of Mum, honestly. It has amazing instructors." Her dad didn't seem to understand that half the appeal was the fact that it *was* a million miles away. Georgie loved their village but at the same time she was desperate to get away. Ever since her mother's accident, she'd been so lonely here. Her dad tried hard, but he didn't know anything about horses, or how it felt to be a thirteen-year-old girl with dreams of horsey super-stardom, stuck in boring old Little Brampton.

Georgie had nothing in common with her dad. Everyone said she was just like her mum, tall and willowy with a fair complexion and smattering of freckles. Her mum had brown hair, though, and Georgie's was blonde. "If I were a pony," Georgie liked to ask her mother, "what colour would I be?"

"Oh, a palomino, I should think," Mrs Parker would reply, "with your beautiful flaxen mane. Not a boring brown mare like your mum."

Georgie was ten years old when Ginny Parker took

the fatal fall that ended her life. The accident happened on the cross-country course at the Blenheim three-star. Ginny Parker had been riding two horses that day. The famed chestnut gelding, The Interloper, generally considered her best horse, and the other her favourite mare, a stunning bay with a white heart-shaped marking on her forehead, whose name was Boudicca.

Mrs Parker always took her daughter to the big competitions. But on this particular weekend Little Brampton was having a gymkhana and so, instead of travelling with her mum, Georgie decided to stay and take Tyro on his first outing. It was a decision she would always regret. If she had known what was going to happen that day she would have been by her mother's side. Instead, when Ginny Parker fell, Georgie was scooping up prizes on Tyro at the gymkhana, completely oblivious to the fact that her life was about to change forever.

No one really knew exactly what happened on the course at Blenheim Palace. Everyone said that Boudicca was going brilliantly, until she reached a fence known as the Blenheim coffin. Ginny Parker had urged the mare over the log at the top of the steep bank, and Boudicca flew the jump with ease, but as she landed, the mare somehow lost her footing. Ginny tried to correct her, but it was too late. Instead of jumping the ditch at the bottom of the bank Boudicca somersaulted into it – with Georgie's mum pinned underneath her.

Ginny Parker's death rocked the whole village. Everybody in Little Brampton knew the Parkers. Not only because Ginny Parker was an internationally renowned rider, but also because Georgie's dad was the local GP.

After the accident, Dr Parker insisted that Boudicca, who had survived the fall, should be sold along with Ginny's other eventing horses. Even worse, he was adamant that Tyro had to go as well. Georgie, having already lost her mother, was about to lose her best friend in the world.

That was when Lucinda Milwood stepped in. Lucinda ran the local riding school just five minutes down the road from the Parkers' cottage. When Georgie turned up there in tears over losing Tyro, Lucinda managed to convince a reluctant Dr Parker to allow her to keep the black gelding at the riding school instead of selling him.

Lucinda's riding school soon became like a second home for Georgie. In exchange for Tyro's board, she went there every morning before school to muck out the stables and groom the ponies to get them ready for the day's lessons. Straight after school, she would change out of her uniform and into her jods to exercise the horses. Afternoons were often busy with riding-school lessons, but if there was time Lucinda would instruct Georgie on Tyro.

Georgie had ridden lots of other horses, but there was something special about Tyro. He was a handsome pony, with a solid, muscular conformation and stocky limbs that made him a jumping machine. His jet-black colouring was unusual for a Connemara, and he had an indefinable presence, a look-at-me quality, that made him stand out in the show ring. The partnership between them really clicked. In three short years Georgie had schooled him up through the grades so that he was one of the best eventing ponies in the district.

In preparation for the Blainford auditions Georgie and Tyro had trained every day. Sometimes, when her schedule had been tight, Georgie had even got up at 5am to ride before school so that she could get the black pony into top shape. But it turned out her efforts were all for nothing. When Tyro went down at the water jump he had taken Georgie's hopes and dreams down with him. She had failed to ace the audition, in fact she had come at the very bottom of the field. Georgie truly believed her chance of a place at Blainford had gone. So she was shocked on Monday afternoon when, not long after she arrived home from school, Lucinda called her on the phone, breathlessly excited.

"I'm down at the stables," Lucinda told her, "come straight away and meet me! And wear your jods!"

Lucinda had hung up before Georgie had the chance to ask what was going on. By the time Georgie arrived at the yard she found Lucinda working Tyro around the arena on the lunge rein. When she caught sight of Georgie she gave her a grin. "He's totally sound!" Lucinda called out. "The accident didn't hurt him at all – he'll be ready to jump in time for the weekend."

27

"Which is great, Lucinda, except we're not entered in anything this weekend." Georgie screwed up her face. "The auditions are over."

"No," Lucinda shook her head. "They're not. There's still one more semi-final audition left. Next weekend in Cirencester."

"Another one-day event?" Georgie was stunned.

"No," Lucinda said. "It's showjumping."

"But I'm not a showjumper!"

Lucinda wouldn't be deterred. "For goodness sake, Georgie, don't be wet! You know how to jump, don't you? Tyro always goes clear in the showjumping phase at one-day events. OK, so he's never jumped as high as a showjumper and he lacks some technique, but we have a week to train him. Isn't it better than just giving up? At least this way you still stand a chance!"

"But I don't want to be a showjumper! I'm an eventer."

Lucinda rolled her eyes. "It doesn't matter! All you have to do is make it through the showjumping audition to get yourself a place at the grand finals. And once the academy accepts you, you can revert back to being an eventing rider."

Georgie's heart was racing. "Is there enough time for me to enter?"

"Already done!" Lucinda said. "Your name is on the audition list. We'll have to leave very early on Saturday to make the drive to Cirencester…" she paused, "…and there is one other tiny detail that might be a problem."

Georgie groaned. "What is it?"

"I've just found out that the head of the Blainford selection panel will be there." Lucinda hesitated. "Have you heard of Tara Kelly?"

"Tara Kelly!" Georgie couldn't believe it. "I remember seeing her on TV when she won the Lexington Horse Trials. She's an amazing rider."

Lucinda nodded. "She's also the head of admissions for Blainford and she's got a reputation for being extremely hard-nosed. One year, she was supposed to take five riders from the UK but she decided only two were up to scratch so she cut the list and left the other three behind."

"OK," Georgie said, "so she's tough. Then Tyro and

I will just have to impress her."

Lucinda hesitated. "There's more to it. The thing is, Tara will be watching you. She knows who you are, you see. Because she knew your mother."

"She knew Mum?" Georgie perked up. "But that's great! If she recognises my name it might help my chances of being selected."

"I doubt it," Lucinda said darkly. "Georgie, when I say that Tara knew Ginny that might not necessarily be a positive thing..."

Georgie was confused. "What are you talking about?"

"That's what I'm trying to tell you," Lucinda said. "Your mother and Tara weren't friends. They were rivals."

Chapter Three

Tara Kelly raced her rental car down the narrow lanes, catching glimpses of the countryside flashing by as she drove at breakneck speed. She had almost forgotten how beautiful England could be in the springtime, the old stone cottages, and apple trees in bloom.

It had been a long time since her last visit. For the past three years another Blainford selector had been responsible for handling the UK while Tara had been re-assigned to the other end of the world, looking for fresh talent in Australia and Japan. This year however, the roster had changed again and Tara had returned to Europe.

Last week she had been in Germany with other selectors for the finals of the European auditions, and they had chosen several excellent new admissions for the academy. The two best new entrants were outstanding dressage riders, which, Tara thought with a wry smile, would no doubt please Bettina Schmidt. Bettina was the head of Blainford's dressage department and had always been critical of the recruitment process for the academy. Bettina's concern was that Tara, as both chief selector and the head of Blainford's eventing department, was biased towards eventing riders. In fact the truth was quite the opposite. As four-times winner of the Lexington Horse Trials, Tara set especially high standards for students applying to join her department.

The selection process was tough no matter what category you applied for. Only the best riders from showjumpers and polo players to Western and natural horsemanship disciples, even vaulters and carriage drivers, were chosen.

Blainford had earned its reputation by maintaining the highest standards and entry to the academy was exclusive. Tara and her team of selectors had to make certain that the right choices were made.

The shortlist of potential applicants crumpled at the bottom of Tara Kelly's brown leather bag was becoming shorter by the day. After the Cirencester show it would become shorter still. 116 junior showjumpers were competing in this last semi-final. Only three of them would make it through to the final auditions next weekend at the Birmingham NEC.

It was impossible of course for Tara to remember the name of every aspiring rider on the shortlist, but there was one that had leapt off the page at her from the very first time she had seen it. That name was Georgina Parker.

✳

"It's not so much that Tara and your mum hated each other," Lucinda explained as she drove the horse lorry into the Cirencester showgrounds. "They were the best riders in the eventing class and there was this constant rivalry. They used their competitiveness with each other to spur themselves on, I suppose. Between them, they won every single prize in their senior year at school."

33

"So why didn't Mum talk about her?" Georgie asked.

"Their lives didn't really connect much after that," Lucinda said. "They both turned professional and for a short while they rode against each other on the international circuit. But then your mum took some time off to have you and when she returned to eventing Tara had given up competing to take up her position at Blainford."

Lucinda stopped talking to concentrate on parking the lorry then said, "Right. I'll go get your registration number while you unload him and saddle up."

Normally at a one-day event, Georgie knew quite a few of the other riders. It was fun to meet up at shows and there would be friendly smiles and chit-chat. But she didn't know a soul at Cirencester and the atmosphere was tense and bristling with competition.

As Georgie unloaded Tyro she felt the stares of the other riders. They were watching, assessing their new rival. Tyro, of course, played to the crowd by high-stepping down the ramp as if he were a race horse arriving at the Grand National. The pony carried himself as if he were a statuesque Thoroughbred stallion instead of a fourteen-two hand gelding. He stood at the bottom of the lorry ramp and utterly embarrassed Georgie by holding his head high in the air and letting out a loud, brazen whinny as if to say "I've arrived! Everyone look at me!"

"Stop being a show-off!" Georgie giggled at his antics. But no one else seemed amused. There were serious faces on all the other riders as they trotted past, eyeing Georgie and Tyro suspiciously.

It got worse once Georgie mounted up and rode Tyro along the avenue of swanky horse lorries and into the practice arena. Here, it was every man for himself as riders kept getting in each other's way as they warmed up. Georgie cantered a bit close to a gangly-legged girl on a pretty grey pony and received a vicious telling-off from the girl's mum who had bleached blonde hair and a strangely orange complexion, which Georgie eventually realised was due to a spray tan and not a hideous skin condition.

"Keep off! You'll make Caprice upset!" the mother complained loudly. "She's very sensitive!"

"I'm sorry, Caprice." Georgie pulled Tyro up to apologise.

"My name is Sybil." The girl looked at Georgie like she was a total idiot. "Caprice is my pony."

"Oh, sorry," Georgie said again. Caprice, meanwhile, had noticed Tyro. She reached her long elegant grey neck out to touch noses with the gelding and, in a gesture typical of stroppy mares, greeted him by giving a sudden, high-pitched squeal and lashing out with a vicious swipe of her foreleg.

"See!" the orange-faced woman fumed. "Now you've gone and upset her!" She snatched Caprice by the reins and dragged the pony and her daughter off to the other side of the field. "If you come near us again I'm reporting you to the officials," she told Georgie loudly.

A girl on a fourteen-two hand palomino had been watching the whole commotion and rode up to Georgie with a smile on her face. "I saw mad Mrs Hawley giving you a hard time," she said. "Don't worry – she shouted at me too before you got here. She's such a bossy old bat!"

"It was like getting told off by a giant bottle of Tango!" Georgie giggled.

The girl smiled. "I'm Olivia," she said leaning down to give the palomino a pat on her glossy neck. "And this is Molly. We're from Blackfriars Pony Club in Northampton."

"Molly is gorgeous," Georgie smiled. "I'm Georgie. This is Tyro."

"Isn't this whole auditions thing so intense?" Olivia groaned. "It's like nobody will even say hello. I've seen at least half a dozen kids here that I usually go to pony club with and they won't even look at me!"

Georgie shrugged. "Everyone's just nervous, I guess. You know, there's so much at stake."

"I know!" Olivia nodded vigorously. "I woke up this morning and felt so ill with nerves I didn't think I'd be able to ride today…"

"Olivia!" A woman wearing a baseball cap and jeans called out across the warm-up arena.

"Oh! That's my mum." Olivia grabbed the reins and turned her palomino on her hindquarters. "I better go," she smiled at Georgie. "See you later! Good luck!"

"You too," Georgie said as she watched Olivia ride off.

"There you are!" Lucinda said when Georgie arrived back at the lorry. "Tie Tyro up with a hay net and come with me. It's time to walk the course."

The fences in the arena looked all right from a distance. It wasn't until you were actually standing next to the jumps that you realised how big they really were.

As Lucinda went from fence to fence, explaining about the best line to take for each jump, Georgie felt her knees gradually turning to jelly beneath her. She'd let Lucinda convince her that there wasn't much between being an eventing rider and a showjumper, forgetting the one key difference – showjumping fences were massive!

Olivia was walking the course with her mum, who turned out to be an old friend of Lucinda's.

"Everyone says that the treble is the bogey fence," Olivia groaned. "It's a totally enormous spread on the last jump."

But Lucinda wasn't so sure. "Sometimes the big ones

38

that look the hardest actually ride easy. Let's wait and see how the others handle it," she told Georgie. "There are thirty-one riders ahead of you so you'll have a chance to see where the problems are."

The first rider into the ring was Byron Montford. Byron rode a glamorous bay hack called Toledo and he had every piece of flashy tack imaginable. None of which stopped him from coming to grief at several of the jumps, including the treble, to rack up a final score of sixteen faults.

"This course is going to be very tough indeed," Lucinda muttered. She was proven right as one after another polished combination of horse and rider entered the ring looking for a clear round and were knocked out by fallen rails or refusals.

"That's the point of these sudden death rounds." Lucinda shrugged. "They're trying to narrow down the competition quickly. Mind you, at this rate hardly anyone will make the jump-offs!"

By the time rider number twenty-five was in the ring, Georgie was back at the lorry tightening Tyro's girth and preparing to mount up. As she adjusted the black pony's noseband she leant in so that her face was right up close. "This is it, Tyro," she whispered. "We've been given another chance to make it to Blainford. Just don't tell anyone you're not a real showjumper, OK? We're going to go in there and fox them and make it through. All you have to do is go clear."

The Connemara cocked one ear to listen as she spoke and Georgie hoped that her pony understood what she was saying. He was a seasoned eventer and was probably expecting business as usual – a dressage test followed by cross-country then showjumping. But today they would be going straight to the showjumping ring. And they'd be going over the biggest fences Tyro had ever jumped in his life.

In the ring competitor number thirty-one, Sybil Hawley, was just completing a round that left the audience with their hearts in their mouths. Sybil had a strange style, galloping wildly between fences and then yanking Caprice in the mouth, before throwing the reins away right before the fence. Poor Caprice! The grey mare was clearly being driven mad by her rider's busy hands and spent most of the round trying to get above the bit, her head held high and the whites of her eyes showing. It was seat-of-the-pants stuff over every jump, but somehow they got through.

"A clear round for Sybil Hawley and Caprice. Can competitor thirty-two, Georgina Parker and Tyro, please enter the arena!" The announcer's voice boomed over the tannoy.

As the two girls rode past each other in opposite directions through the narrow entrance to the arena, Georgie gave Sybil a smile but it wasn't returned. When she recalled this later, Georgie thought she saw Sybil out of the corner of her eye, surreptitiously raising her whip. She didn't see what happened next, but suddenly Tyro had shot forward underneath her, bolting into the arena. Did Sybil hit Tyro with her whip? All Georgie knew was that Tyro was calm one moment and then he'd gone like a rocket.

"Hoi! Tyro!" Georgie was so totally focused on hanging on to her pony she had completely stopped paying attention to the loudspeaker. When she finally had Tyro settled into a steady canter, she noticed that the warbling banter which normally poured out

41

through the tannoy between rounds had stopped. There was only deafening silence as the crowd waited for her round to begin. Georgie began to panic. Had they rung the bell to start and she hadn't noticed? Had she missed her cue? She wasn't very experienced at showjumping but she knew that if they had rung the bell, then she only had a minute to cross the start line or she would be eliminated! She looked around at the audience, trying to find Lucinda. There was no sign of her trainer and still no sound from the loudspeaker. They must have rung the bell already!

In a mad panic, Georgie turned Tyro and headed back up the arena towards the start line. She did a quick loop at a brisk canter and then rode the black pony forward. She was half a stride over the line when she heard the bell ring out. She hadn't missed it after all! Well, that was fine now – she was off!

At the first jump, Tyro's stride was too long and he leapt from too far back. Georgie was certain that he would drop his hind legs over the back rails and drop a pole, but he only contacted the rail gently with his fetlocks and the pole stayed in its cup.

At fence two she was back in control and rode the pony perfectly into the jump, taking it neatly. Tyro gave a little buck, flinging his legs up in high spirits as if to say, "piece of cake!"

By the time they reached the bogey fence, the treble, Georgie had hit her stride. The final spread was really huge and she felt her tummy tie up in nervous knots, but she did what any good rider does when they are scared – she kicked on. "Come on!" she shouted at Tyro. He lifted up into the air and took the jump. They were still clear!

Then before she could even think about it, she was over the green plank upright and the last jump, a wide oxer made of pale blue rails, and then Georgie was through the flags and the crowd was clapping. It was the third clear round of the day!

"Oh well done! Well done!" Lucinda raced up to her as she emerged from the arena.

"He was genius, wasn't he?" Georgie enthused. "Did you see the way he took the treble?"

"You were both brilliant!" Lucinda told her with a huge grin on her face. "You're through to the next round."

"I don't think so!" a voice boomed out. Georgie looked up and saw the orange face of Mrs Hawley bearing down on them. If Mrs Hawley had looked thunderous earlier in the practice ring, now she looked positively volcanic.

"You're a cheat!"

These words were said with such venom that Georgie and Lucinda were dumbstruck. Unfortunately, Mrs Hawley wasn't and she continued with her vicious rant. "I've reported you to the selector!" Mrs Hawley raved. "I'm going to see to it that you are eliminated!"

"What are you talking about?" Lucinda Milwood was baffled.

"Your daughter broke across the start line before the bell," Mrs Hawley snarled. "Everyone saw it."

"She's not my daughter," Lucinda corrected her, "and this round wasn't being judged on time. Who cares if she crossed the line early?"

"It's against the rules!" Mrs Hawley's face was puce with rage beneath the orange tan. "The girl should be eliminated from the competition. You'll see! I've already taken this to the highest level. The selector is on her way over here now!"

Through the crowds came a slender woman wearing dove grey jodhpurs and a navy blouse, her walnut-brown hair held back by a pair of stylish black sunglasses.

Mrs Hawley looked smug as the selector approached. The smugness rapidly vanished when the woman in grey jodhpurs took one look at Lucinda Milwood, shrieked with delight and gave her an enormous hug.

"Lucy!" she exclaimed. "My God! Lucy Milwood! It's been such a long time, but you haven't changed one bit!"

Georgie's trainer laughed. "You neither! It's so good to see you!"

Mrs Hawley was gasping like a goldfish. This was not the result she had been hoping for.

The selector ignored Mrs Hawley and turned her attention to Georgie. "So this must be Ginny's daughter?" She had a strange expression on her face as she stared hard at Georgie. "You are the spitting image

45

of your mother. Let's hope you can ride like her as well."

"Georgie," Lucinda smiled, "I'd like you to meet the only rider who ever beat your mother around the cross-country course at Blainford Academy.

"Say hello to Tara Kelly."

Chapter Four

The fact that Tara and Lucinda were clearly old friends only made matters worse as far as Mrs Hawley was concerned.

"Blatant favouritism!" she fumed.

Tara Kelly had been chief selector at Blainford for long enough to know how to handle pushy parents. "Mrs Hawley," she said firmly, "as Blainford's chief of admissions and head selector, I can assure you that I am completely impartial at all times."

Mrs Hawley had a malicious glint in her eye. "So does that mean you'll disqualify her?"

"The rules clearly state that if a rider in any way gains an advantage by crossing the line before the bell then they will be disqualified," Tara said.

47

Georgie felt her heart pounding in her ears. This couldn't be happening. It was bad enough to lose her chance of going to Blainford with that freak accident at the water jump. Now, to be eliminated again because of some crazy rule! Georgie looked at Sybil who was smiling wickedly from behind Tara's back and waggling her whip at her.

"But I didn't hear the bell," Georgie protested, "it wasn't my fault."

Tara ignored her. "As I was saying," she continued, "riders are disqualified if they have gained an advantage by crossing the line early. But since this round wasn't a jump-off against the clock the time didn't matter. Georgie gained nothing by crossing the line early."

"So...?" Mrs Hawley bristled.

"There will be no elimination. She's going through to the next round."

Mrs Hawley stomped off angrily as Tara looked at her watch. "I'd better get back to the selectors' tent," she said. "There are still sixty riders to get through the first phase before lunch break."

"Why don't you come and meet us at my lorry for lunch?" Lucinda offered.

Tara shook her head. "I don't think that would be wise. We don't want to give the Mrs Hawleys of this world a chance to cry favouritism again, do we?" The chief selector turned to Georgie. "I'm surprised to see you here today, Georgina. I didn't think Ginny's daughter would be a showjumper."

"I'm an eventer, really," Georgie said, "at least, I want to be one."

"Good!" Tara said brightly. "So if you make it through the auditions I can look forward to having you in my cross-country classes."

Georgie felt quite pleased until Tara added, "It's the toughest course at Blainford. If a rider isn't good enough they're gone. Only half the students who start the year with me will make it through to the end. It's dangerous too – the cross-country department holds the record for more broken bones than the rest of the school put together. Perhaps you might like to reconsider and take up showjumping – it's a much safer option."

49

And with that, Tara waved a brisk goodbye and headed back to the selectors' tent. Georgie was wide-eyed as she watched her go. "Broken bones? Is she running a cross-country class or Accident and Emergency?"

Lucinda sighed. "Don't be put off. Tara loves to come across as icy and strict when in fact she's..." Lucinda paused. "Well, actually, that's pretty much what she's like. She's a perfectionist – and at her peak she was ranked one of the best riders in the world. She's a brilliant teacher. If you're lucky enough to get into her class at Blainford you should jump at the chance."

✳

Although Tara turned down Lucinda's offer of lunch, they had company as Olivia and her mum came over to join them. For dessert Mrs Prescott brought jam tarts and Lucinda produced her irresistible ginger crunch.

Olivia had two slices and then pronounced that the butterflies in her tummy now felt even worse than before.

"I've eaten too much! I won't make it through in the

jump-offs," she groaned as she lay back on the ramp of the lorry holding her tummy.

"Yes," Georgie agreed, "it was my cunning plan to invite you over to scoff all the ginger crunch."

Olivia and Molly had put in a very professional round that morning, jumping the course so smoothly and cleanly they made it look easy, which it wasn't. From the total pool of 116 riders, only a meagre fourteen had made it through to the next round. The rest were packing their horses into their lorries and trailers for the drive home.

"I can't believe Sybil Hawley got through," Georgie groaned. "Did you hear her mum shrieking on the sidelines?"

Olivia giggled, "Poor Sybil. I'd hate to have a mum like that."

"What, noisy?" Georgie said.

"No, orange!" Olivia burst out laughing. Georgie collapsed with the giggles too. It had been really good fun hanging out with Olivia today. Georgie hoped that they would both make it through to the finals in Birmingham.

✳

51

The next round that afternoon was a speed contest and the jumps had been raised to a metre twenty. Georgie was feeling confident about riding against the clock. Tyro was the fastest pony she had ever ridden and he was brilliant at tight turns. Georgie had walked the course and was planning on taking some very tricky, extreme shortcuts. The last two jumps were key for Georgie's alternative route, cutting a corner to come in at the planks on a sharp angle. If they could pull it off this might slash their time by two whole seconds. It was a risky strategy, but worth it if they went clear.

At 2pm there was a briefing in the main arena for the remaining fourteen riders. They were told to arrive with their horses fully tacked up. "What is this about?" Georgie asked.

Lucinda frowned. "I'm not sure, but the selectors often like to throw a curve ball at this phase to test the riders. One year they made everyone take off their saddles and compete bareback."

Georgie looked at the enormous jumps in the arena. It would be a nightmare trying to ride a course like that bareback! Surely the selectors weren't planning the same thing?

As the riders organised themselves, Tara Kelly walked into the arena and stood in front of them. "Can all the riders please dismount and run up your stirrups," she announced. "We're going to make some last minute changes."

Georgie dismounted nervously. She felt her palms sweating as she gripped the reins. As Tara Kelly strode back and forth with arms folded across her chest, Georgie felt sick with anticipation, certain that at any moment they would be instructed to remove their saddles. But this year Blainford's chief selector had another trial in mind.

"I know how hard you have trained to be here," Tara said. "You've schooled your ponies and become a team." She paused. "I want to see what happens when that team is torn apart."

Tara stepped forward and began walking down the line-up, handing each rider a folded-over piece of paper. "A great rider should be able to mount up on any horse and achieve a clear round," Tara continued as she walked along handing out the papers. "This afternoon we'll be testing your abilities on a horse that you've never ridden before."

Tara handed out the last two to Olivia and Georgie."On your piece of paper you'll find the name of one of the horses in this arena." Tara paused. "That's the horse you'll ride for the next round. As of right now, you are swapping mounts. The names have been chosen at random. There can be no complaints and no trading. You must ride the horse you have been given. The rules of the competition remain the same – a clear round in the fastest time will win. Two refusals in this round and you are out." Tara looked at the line-up of stunned faces. "Please open your piece of paper."

Georgie unfolded hers and felt her stomach lurch in shock.

Tara continued, "You may go and claim the horse." No one moved. "Hurry up and find your horses!" Tara told them. "The first rider is due to jump in twenty minutes."

The fourteen riders suddenly began running in all directions, dragging their horses behind them in a mad rush as they frantically searched for the horse they had been drawn to ride. Georgie hadn't moved. She was staring at the paper in disbelief. She had drawn Caprice.

✳

"Any tips for riding her?" Georgie asked as she walked over to take Sybil's horse.

"You must be joking!" Sybil virtually flung the reins at her. "I'm not giving you any help!"

At least Sybil hadn't been allocated Tyro, Georgie thought as she stood holding two horses. She was dreading handing over her beloved pony to some complete stranger and kept an anxious watch on anyone who approached her. Georgie was beyond relieved when Olivia came up positively beaming, waving Tyro's name on her slip.

"I can't believe I got him!" Olivia said. "Isn't this the craziest thing you've ever seen?"

Her hands were shaking as she took Tyro's reins. "I've had Molly for two years," she explained. "I haven't been on another horse for ages."

"Tyro won't give you any trouble," Georgie reassured her. "He never refuses a jump, but he does rush fences sometimes so sit back between them."

"OK." Olivia was trying to take deep breaths. "I can do that."

"He's fast too," Georgie said, stroking the Connemara's pretty face, "and he's good at correcting his own stride. Give him his head once you hit the treble and he'll be fine."

"Thanks!" Olivia said and smiled at Georgie. "I know he's special. Don't worry. I'll look after him, I promise."

Lucinda was thrilled with the horse-swap challenge. "I watched this mare jump in the last round. She's very schooled and she's got talent," she said, adjusting the stirrups to fit Georgie's legs which were much shorter than Sybil's. "If Caprice can pull off a clear round with Sybil on her back then I'm sure you can get a clear round out of her too."

Any reservations Georgie had about swapping horses disappeared once she was up on Caprice. She was a very positive pony with big paces and when

Georgie popped her over the practice jump the mare had her ears pricked and cantered on eagerly, taking the fence off a lovely forward stride.

As the riders warmed up, their names and numbers were called over the loudspeaker. Georgie was last to go. She didn't know if this was good or bad. She had more time to warm up, but also more time to get nervous.

"Could rider number one, Ellie Trainor, please enter the ring," the announcer called. Georgie watched as a girl on a strawberry roan came into the collection area looking tense. That morning the same girl had done a beautiful clear round on a bay mare, but as she rode at the first jump she seemed to lose her nerve and the strawberry roan slammed on the brakes and skidded into the fence. The girl gave a half-hearted whack with her crop and swung the horse around to try again. But the roan had lost confidence in her rider and had no intention of trying to jump. She gave an outright refusal, propping and baulking, and the bell rang. The first rider had been eliminated.

On the sidelines Lucinda frowned. "You must ride at

the fences as if you really mean it, Georgie. If you're half-hearted Caprice will sense your hesitation and you'll fail."

As each of the riders squared up to the first jump you could tell by the look on their face whether they would make it or not. There were some awful crashes as riders lost their bottle and ponies ploughed into jumps with last minute refusals. One of these riders was Sybil Hawley. The chestnut pony she was riding made a sudden stop in front of the jump – and Sybil didn't. She flew over the pony's neck and landed without a horse beneath her, on her bottom on the other side of the fence. Mrs Hawley would protest of course, but Sybil's audition was well and truly over.

By the time Olivia and Tyro were up there had been no clear rounds at all. The best scores so far belonged to two riders with eight faults each. It was beginning to look like no one could make it clear on an unknown horse.

"Come on, Olivia!" Georgie called out from the sidelines. It was the strangest sensation, watching her own pony competing without her. Georgie felt a brief moment of anguish as she watched Tyro take the first jump with ease and desperately wished she were the one on his back. But Olivia rode him beautifully and when they took the last fence for the first clear round, Georgie was clapping louder than anyone.

"You should be proud of that round," Lucinda told Georgie.

"But I wasn't the one riding!" Georgie said.

"No, but you trained him. You've schooled Tyro well and it shows. He's a credit to you."

Olivia was totally smitten. "He is the most amazing pony," she gushed to Georgie. "I know I'm being really cheeky saying this but if you ever decide to sell Tyro, will you please call me? I'd love to buy him!"

After Olivia went clear, the floodgates opened and by Georgie's turn to ride there had been five clear rounds. To make the top three Georgie not only had to go clear, she also had to get a quick-smart time to beat the others on the clock.

It was a fine line to tread. If she went hell for leather then she risked making a mistake. All it would take was a single refusal or a rail down to totally blow her chances. But if she went too cautiously she might lose on time faults.

As she entered the arena Georgie urged Caprice into a steady canter and stood up in her stirrups in two-point position. She rode a lap around the fences, mentally mapping her route between the jumps. So far, no one had taken the shortcut that she'd been planning to take on Tyro. Should she risk it on an unknown horse or aim for a safe, clear round and hope her time would be good enough?

This time she heard the bell ring loud and clear. With a tip of her hat to the selectors, she rode one last lap around the perimeter and then came through the flags like a rocket. The clock was ticking. She had to go clear and make every second count.

Georgie rode at the first fence with almost too much energy and Caprice took off from too far back with a huge stride. Her hind legs scraped the rail and Georgie heard the crowd go "ohhh!" as the pole rocked in its cups. But it didn't fall. She steadied the mare and took her time over the next few fences. Through the treble one... two... three! Georgie had got the striding perfect on the jumps but she sensed that their time was far too slow. There were only two fences left. If Georgie wanted to beat the other clear rounds, she had to go for the shortcut.

Over number eight she had to virtually twist Caprice in mid-air, so that the mare landed at an angle. There was a gasp from the crowd as they realised what Georgie was doing and another as Caprice nearly hit a fence as she swerved to the right. Then, suddenly, the last jump loomed right in front of Georgie. She would almost have to jump it sideways to make it over.

Georgie took a deep breath and kicked on. Caprice put in one last stride and then lifted up into the air. There was a choked silence from the crowd. Would she get over? The turn had been so tight it seemed like an impossible leap.

Georgie had judged it like a pro! Caprice flew the fence with room to spare. As she landed on the other side the wild applause told Georgie all she needed to know. She had done it. Georgie was on her way to the finals.

Chapter Five

The crowd in the grandstand of Birmingham's NEC Arena was buzzing with a sense of anticipation. They had already marvelled at the thrills and spills of the scurry races, and gasped at the fantastic Lipizzaner stunt horses performing *Swan Lake*.

"We do hope you've enjoyed the entertainment so far," announcer Mike Partridge warbled to the audience. "Now it's time for the main event. You're about to see the very best young talent in Britain take the ride of their lives. It's the grand final of the Blainford Academy auditions!"

The crowd gave a cheer and Mike Partridge continued his introduction. "The riders performing for us today are no older than thirteen years of age. All have passed rigorous tests to prove they're the best in their chosen field. We've got eventers and showjumpers, polo players and dressage riders and we've even got a Western rider and natural horsemanship star making an appearance!

"Twenty young hopefuls competing for just five places. It's the competition of a lifetime for these kids." Mike Partridge paused. "We'll meet the first of our twenty finalists in just a moment, but before we do that, let me introduce you to our selectors!"

Three giant spotlights flashed on to the arena, tracing circles of light across the golden sand before concentrating on the three judges sitting at the selectors' table at the far end of the arena.

"Our first selector is a household name – winner of countless Horse of the Year titles, a showjumping superstar and the glamour girl of the British Olympic equestrian squad – it's the one and only Helen Nicholson!"

The crowd cheered louder than ever as a very beautiful woman with dark brown hair, big brown eyes and a warm smile got up to give them a wave.

"Our next selector," Mike Partridge began, "is an

animal behaviourist whose books on horse training have sold millions. He's also an Australian – but don't hold that against him! Ladies and gentlemen – it's Dr David McGee!" A handsome grey-haired man stood up and waved to the crowd who clapped politely.

"And finally," Mike Partridge continued, "a woman who needs no introduction. Blainford's senior selector is an international eventing superstar and a four-times winner of the Lexington Horse Trials. She's a serious horsewoman – I should know, I've been trying all morning to get her to smile! Let's give her a round of applause and see if she'll give us a grin... Please welcome Tara Kelly!"

Tara Kelly gritted her teeth at the announcer's sense of humour. Although it was her job to judge the finals, she had never really got used to the crowds, the lights and the theatrics that came with the event. Over the years, Blainford's auditions had become more and more spectacular and grand finals night was now so renowned, it had become one of the most exciting events on the British equestrian calendar. All a bit over the top in Tara Kelly's opinion, but despite her reservations she went along with it because as Blainford's headmistress, Mrs Dickins-Thomson, pointed out to her, it was brilliant publicity for the school.

"C'mon, Tara, give us a wave, luv!" Mike Partridge coaxed and Tara rose from her seat and grinned and waved at the crowds in the stands. They were here to see a show after all.

Besides, in some ways the three-ring circus that had grown up around the event was a good thing, Tara reasoned. It added to the pressure and gave the twenty candidates waiting backstage a very real taste of what life was like under the spotlight. If you really wanted to be an international horse-riding superstar then these final auditions were a good test of character. Could the twenty riders all stay cucumber-cool when thousands were watching them and Mike Partridge was singing their praises over the loudspeaker?

Until now, the auditions had been divided into separate categories for eventers, showjumpers, dressage riders and so on. But the finals brought all the different disciplines together. With so many different kinds of riders auditioning, it wouldn't be fair to rely on a single test to compare their skills. Instead, each of the twenty riders was required to create a freestyle performance. They would all have fifteen minutes in the arena and the selectors would cast votes with score cards.

Tara trusted her fellow judges. Helen and David were both experienced and had done the job alongside her before. She would listen carefully to their opinions but at the end of the day they knew that the final choice would always be hers.

"You've met our three selectors," Mike Partridge called out. "Now, let's meet our first finalist. She's a dressage rider from Dundee and at only eleven years old she's one of the youngest competitors today. She's going to be performing a freestyle dressage kur for us on her lovely pony The Cheshire Cat. Here she is, Miss Sally Stevens!"

The music began, the lights came up and a very pretty skewbald pony entered the ring. He flew down the centre of the arena in a floating, extended trot and then halted in front of the judges. His rider, a slightly built girl in a blue showing jacket and banana jods, gave a stiff salute and then set off again at a collected canter.

Backstage, hidden by large black screens from the view of the audience, nineteen young riders watched Sally anxiously and waited for their turn in the spotlight.

"Are you nervous?" Olivia hissed. She was standing beside Georgie, gripping on to Molly's reins and looking terrified.

"Uh-huh," Georgie said. She was trying to stay focused, but it wasn't easy because her dad had dropped a bombshell about her future.

Over dinner the weekend before the grand finals Georgie was telling her dad about her plans for the performance. "We've come up with something super-special to grab the selectors' attention," she said.

"Mmmm," her father nodded absentmindedly.

Georgie rolled her eyes. "Tyro is going to wear a ballerina tutu and we'll be doing a tango. It's *Strictly Come Dancing* except with ponies."

"That's great, honey."

"Dad! I was totally joking! Are you even listening to me? Do you care that I'm in the finals?"

This was so typical! It was the most exciting thing to happen to her ever, and her father hardly seemed to be paying attention.

"I'm sorry, Georgie," Dr Parker sighed, "I... The thing is... we need to talk."

"Uh-oh," Georgie said. "Is this going to be a serious conversation?"

Dr Parker wasn't smiling. "It's about the auditions. And yes, it's serious I'm afraid." Georgie's face fell. "I know you've got your heart set on going to Blainford," her dad began, "but the fees are steep, Georgie, it's a very expensive private school."

"I know that," Georgie's voice had an edge of panic, "but Mum already put the money aside years ago. You told me she did!"

"Yes, that's true," her dad said.

"So what's the problem?" Georgie asked.

Her dad hesitated, and then finally spoke. "She put aside your fees. But she didn't put aside enough for Tyro."

"What do you mean?"

"I mean there's no money for your horse to go with you," Dr Parker said.

"How much does it cost?"

"Ten thousand a term – and that's just for Tyro's board. Then there's the shipping costs of transporting him to Lexington." Dr Parker shook his head. "I'm a country GP, Georgie, not some Harley Street physician. We just don't have that kind of money."

"This is because you don't want me to go, isn't it?" Georgie couldn't help herself, she was so upset she was shaking. "You've never wanted me to go to Blainford! And now I've qualified for the finals, and this is just your way of wiggling out of it!"

"I can understand why you'd think that, Georgie, but it simply isn't true. And that's not what I'm saying. You can go to Blainford." Dr Parker looked at his daughter. "But if you go, Georgie, it will be without Tyro."

"She's brilliant, isn't she?" Olivia hissed to Georgie, shaking her back to reality. Sally Stevens and The

69

Cheshire Cat had nearly finished their performance. They floated across the arena in a lovely canter and performed several perfect flying changes, completed their display with a very tidy *piaffe*, saluting in front of the judges. The crowd went wild with applause.

"What a marvellous performance!" Mike Partridge enthused. "Come on then, Helen Nicholson! Let's hear your thoughts."

Helen grinned at Sally who was pink-cheeked and exhausted. "That was brilliant!" she said brightly in a thick Yorkshire accent. "Great half-passes, a really super extended trot and your pony was looking through the bridle the whole time." She lifted up her score card. "I'm giving you an eight!" The crowd cheered.

"David McGee," said the announcer, "can we have your score please?"

"I liked the way you and your pony were working together. Nice paces, nice attitude, you really had him on the bit the whole time," David McGee said as he raised his number. "I loved it and I'm giving you a nine!" The crowd whooped even louder. Then Tara Kelly cleared her throat and spoke into her microphone.

"Sally," she said coolly, "dressage is supposed to be graceful. Your performance felt a bit rushed and almost jerky to me."

The crowd went silent. A couple of people booed as Sally's cheery smile began to droop. But Tara continued.

"Not enough energy, not enough presence. I felt like the whole performance lacked impulsion and oomph..."

There were more boos now and a woman in the crowd shouted out defiantly, "We love you, Sally!" Tara Kelly ignored her and finished what she had to say. "You're eleven years old, and it shows. You need another year under your belt before you audition again. This will not be your year, Sally." Tara held up her score card. "I'm giving you a five."

"Ladies and gentlemen – love her or loathe her, Tara Kelly is our own Simon Cowell, isn't she?" Mike Partridge tried to lighten the mood. "She's given a score of five for little Sally! Now the competition really gets serious as competitor number two enters the arena. She's a natural horsemanship disciple all the way from Herefordshire. Put your hands together for Lauren White!"

Lauren White rode her blanket-spotted Appaloosa into the arena bareback. She had no bridle either, instead she guided the Appaloosa with nothing more than a thin rope cord lashed around the horse's neck.

"Wow!" Olivia said. "I want to see this."

Georgie shook her head. "We don't have time to watch her. We have to go!"

Georgie wasn't a circus performer or a stunt rider. When she found out that she would have to perform a routine she was stumped. How could she capture the selectors' attention and show off her skills? She was thrilled when Olivia phoned her up with a suggestion.

"Maybe we could perform together," Olivia told her. "We could do some sort of double act."

"Is that allowed?" Georgie asked.

"Absolutely – I checked the rules," Olivia confirmed. "Two of us in the arena will make a bigger impression.

If we could figure out some sort of synchronised routine it could be really cool!"

Georgie thought about it. In fact, she realised that she had a brilliant idea for their performance! Olivia loved it and immediately agreed.

So on the week before the Birmingham finals, Georgie and Lucinda loaded Tyro into the horse lorry and moved him from Little Brampton to Olivia's home in Northampton. The two girls would spend the week at Olivia's house, training like mad to perfect their routine.

Olivia had told Georgie there would be good facilities at her place, but Georgie was shocked when she arrived.

"Ohmygod! You live here?" Georgie said when Olivia opened the door. "I thought I'd pressed the doorbell on Balmoral Castle by mistake."

"Sorry," Olivia said, letting her in. "I should have warned you, our house is a bit over the top."

The Prescotts' house was one of the grandest mansions in Northampton, a vast stately residence on over a thousand acres of farmland. The red brick house had eleven bedrooms and a guest cottage where Georgie and Lucinda would stay for the week. Out the back of the main house was an elegant stable block and a huge, landscaped training manège.

Olivia seemed pleasantly oblivious to her family's wealth. As far as she was concerned, all that mattered was horses. She adored Molly almost as much as Georgie loved Tyro. And she worked hard at her riding too. For the entire week it was nothing but long hours of training. And now their time had finally arrived.

In the arena at the Birmingham NEC four finalists had been and gone and not a single one had been given decent points by Blainford's chief selector. Tara's highest mark so far had been a grudging six.

"Let's hope that the next two girls have better luck!" Mike Partridge said breezily. "These riders only just met a week ago at the showjumping semi-finals in Cirencester. Since then, they've become firm friends and will perform together in the arena for us today. You're about to witness something very special," he continued. "The tandem puissance!"

In the arena, three jumps had been built. There was

an upright rail jump constructed from blue striped poles and an oxer made from red ones. Far bigger than both of these fences however, was an enormous wall in the centre of the ring, constructed from giant wooden blocks painted to look like brick.

"You all know the drill, ladies and gentlemen!" Mike Partridge trilled. "That brick wall is the big one. It's going to get higher and higher every time they jump it."

Most of the audience had seen an ordinary puissance before. But this was puissance with a difference. "Normally the wall is jumped one rider at a time. But today these two young riders are trying a daredevil feat. They're going to attempt a dual jump, riding together over the puissance wall!"

There was a gasp of astonishment from the crowd and even Tara Kelly suddenly sat bolt upright and alert.

"Are the jump stewards ready?" Mike Partridge asked. "Excellent! Then please welcome our two daredevil finalists... Olivia Prescott and Georgina Parker!"

Barrelling into the arena at a spanking canter, came

Olivia and Georgie. They had plaited red ribbons into Molly and Tyro's manes and tails so that the palomino and the black pony matched each other beautifully. Both were the same size, fourteen-two, and it was fairly easy for the girls to keep the horses neck and neck as they cantered briskly around the perimeter.

They had been practising so hard it came as second nature to keep their ponies in perfect time with each other. Tyro, who had the slightly bigger stride, was ridden on the outside, while Olivia kept the pressure on Molly to keep pace with the black gelding.

After a lap to say hello to the crowds, the girls steadied the ponies back to a collected canter, and then turned left and rode hard at the first fence. Over the upright rail they went – both ponies taking off into the air at precisely the same time. Then they were turning the corner to the right and cantering on to the next fence, the oxer. Again, the ponies lifted up into the air side by side, precisely on cue.

"This is beautiful co-ordinated riding," Mike Partridge was saying in hushed tones to the crowd. "Both of these riders are thirteen years old. Olivia is from Northampton and Georgie hails from the village of Little Brampton in Gloucestershire. Now, as they come up to the puissance wall, can they keep it together and get over? This is a big wall, ladies and gentlemen. One metre forty! Almost as tall as these two girls who are attempting it. Here they go!"

Without hesitation, Georgie and Olivia kicked on and the black pony and the palomino arced up together and cleared the massive brick wall with ease. They landed neatly on the other side and the crowd went crazy!

"Super stuff!" Mike Partridge raved. "Lovely riding by Georgie and Olivia!"

In the arena, the ground crew were hard at work, slotting a new line of bricks into the top of the jump to make the wall higher for the second round.

"If you thought it was big before, take a look now," Mike Partridge said gaily. "One metre fifty-five. I can tell you it takes a brave rider to tackle a fence that size!"

As Georgie and Olivia rode back into the arena the crowd clapped and cheered louder than before. The girls set off once more at a canter, popping the ponies in perfect time together over the upright and the oxer and then turning once more to face the wall.

As they approached this time, Georgie felt the knot of nerves in her stomach tighten. Although she had jumped this high in their practice sessions, here in the main arena under the lights it somehow seemed monstrous. She cast a quick sideways glance at Olivia, who was pushing Molly on, trying to keep pace with Tyro and prepare herself for the jump that lay ahead.

Two strides out from the fence Georgie stopped worrying about timing and became totally focused on just one thing – getting over the wall. She put her legs on firmly to let Tyro know she meant business and the black gelding responded brilliantly. He leapt and Georgie felt that incredible surge of energy as they rose into the air. It was the most amazing feeling in the world, almost as if they were flying.

Her perfect moment was shattered by gasps of horror from the crowd and a piercing shriek beside her. Molly and Olivia had completely misjudged the fence and instead of going up alongside Tyro, the palomino had barrelled straight into the wall, striking the jump with spectacular force. Molly lurched forward, legs scrambling, and Olivia was thrown from the saddle. Georgie, meanwhile, was in mid-air trying to jump over the now-collapsing tumble of giant wooden blocks falling apart right beneath her horse's belly. There was no way she could stop what was happening. The wall was crashing down, taking Georgie and Tyro with it.

Chapter Six

Reacting on pure adrenalin, Georgie pulled hard on Tyro's right rein so that the gelding changed course and landed further to the right, managing to skirt the fallen bricks and land on the sand surface of the arena. Unbalanced by this sudden twist in mid-air, Tyro hit the ground hard and stumbled forward. Georgie was unseated and found herself in front of the saddle with her arms wrapped around the pony's neck.

Most other riders would have simply fallen off, but Georgie had the nimble athleticism of a cat. She managed somehow to hoist herself back off Tyro's neck and into the saddle, pulling on the reins to get the pony's head up. Then she regained her stirrups and hauled Tyro roughly to a halt at the end of the arena.

Despite his awful stumble, Tyro seemed unharmed. Olivia and Molly, however, were not so lucky. The paramedics were in the arena with Olivia. She had fallen hard and been winded as she struck the ground, but incredibly she had avoided being trampled. When Georgie saw the medics helping her friend stand up she knew Olivia would be OK. It was Molly who had come off the worst. The mare had come down right on top of the fallen bricks. She had injured one of her forelegs quite badly and was clearly lame.

Mrs Prescott and Lucinda raced forward to meet Olivia as she came backstage. "I'm fine," Olivia insisted, shaking her head in disgust at her performance. "I'm just so furious with myself. It was my fault. We were coming towards the wall and I should have pushed Molly on harder but I lost my nerve and hesitated, then she got her striding wrong and crashed right into it!"

"It was just bad luck," Georgie tried to tell Olivia.

"No," Olivia disagreed. "It was bad riding. It's my fault we've failed our audition."

The wall and the other jumps had already been

deconstructed and ferried away and the next rider was entering the ring to begin their round.

While Lucinda led the horses away to their stalls, Mrs Prescott took the girls over to the café near the warm-up arena. She sat them down at one of the plastic tables and bought them both a piece of cake and a cup of tea. "You're in shock, you need some sugar," Mrs Prescott said.

Olivia still looked deathly pale. And she was obviously racked with guilt about ruining their chances. "I'm so sorry," Olivia groaned, "I can't believe I messed it up for you."

"It's OK," Georgie insisted. "Honestly, it's no big deal. Even if I had got in, I probably wasn't going to be able to go to Blainford anyway."

Olivia looked shocked. "Why not?"

Georgie was about to explain when she realised there was a woman standing over their table. She looked very official and was holding a clipboard.

"Excuse me!" the woman said. "Is one of you Georgina Parker?"

Georgie looked up. "I am."

"The selectors asked me to come and find you. They'd like you to come to the judges' table, please."

Georgie looked at Olivia who gave her a shrug.

"Now, please!" the woman said, setting a brisk pace for Georgie to follow as she wound her way from the café through the backstage corridors that led to the other end of the stadium where the selectors were sitting.

When they got there, Georgie had to wait in the wings for a moment while one of the other finalists finished their performance. Then, after the crowd finished clapping and the selectors delivered their verdict and scores, the woman hustled her forward to stand in front of Tara Kelly.

"Georgie Parker." Tara looked her up and down. "There always seems to be some drama to sort out whenever you're around."

Georgie was about to say that really, while this was true, it was hardly her fault. But Tara continued. "The judges have discussed your situation, and we feel that even though you entered as a partnership with Olivia Prescott, it is only fair, since you cleared the wall in the last round, to let you continue the puissance on your own."

Georgie couldn't believe it. "I'm still in?"

"You are most definitely still in, Miss Parker," Dr McGee spoke up. "You cleared the wall and should be allowed to continue. We've put you at the end of the running order to give you time to prepare yourself again."

Georgie didn't know what to say. "Thank you..." she began. Then the lights came on in the arena and the next rider was being announced, and the woman with the clipboard was escorting Georgie away backstage.

Georgie walked to the horse lorry in stunned disbelief. She found Olivia, Lucinda and Mrs Prescott standing by Molly's stall. The vet had just been and diagnosed the condition of Molly's injured leg.

"The good news is it's not broken," Olivia said looking relieved. "The vet thinks the tendon on the cannon bone may have ripped. He's going to give Molly a proper examination when we get her home but he says that she'll need to be spelled for the rest of the season to recover.

"Anyway," Olivia added, "what did the selectors want? Why did they call you over?"

"They've given us a second chance," Georgie told her.

Olivia was stunned. "You mean we can ride again?"

Georgie shook her head. "No. Not you and me. I meant me and Tyro. They're going to let us continue the puissance on our own."

Olivia's face dropped. "Oh, I see."

Georgie felt so stupid! "You know what?" she said to Olivia. "I'm going to go back and tell them I don't want to do it. We're a team. We either do this together or not at all."

But Olivia shook her head. "Don't be silly," she said, taking a deep breath. "This is the best news, Georgie!" she insisted. "I couldn't ride again even if I wanted to – Molly is lame. And you deserve to have another chance. I've been feeling dreadful knowing that I'm responsible for ruining your opportunity to get in to Blainford. It's brilliant that you're still in with a shot." She gave Georgie a big hug. "Good luck," she said sincerely. "I'll be back here, cheering you on."

Lucinda was thrilled that Georgie was being allowed a second go. "Are you sure you're OK about jumping the wall again?" she asked. "It got quite hairy in there when Olivia crashed. You don't have to do this."

"I know," Georgie nodded. "It's all right. Tyro had cleared the wall before it began to fall. He only got a little bit spooked when the bricks collapsed. He'll be fine."

"What about you?" Lucinda said.

Georgie had been more shaken by her almost-accident in the arena than she wanted to admit. But the best way to get over it was to put it out of her mind and continue with the competition. She wished she could go back into the arena straight away. Tyro was ready to jump, his blood was up. Instead, she would have to wait in the collecting ring and somehow remain calm until all the other competitors had their turn.

She could see Daisy King warming up on her big grey Irish Hunter, Village Voice. The two girls had ridden against each other for years on the eventing circuit and often it would be a battle between them for first place. You would have thought they would be friends, but in fact they seldom spoke. Georgie had tried to be friendly but Daisy was very competitive and didn't allow herself any distractions, so Georgie was surprised when Daisy popped her horse over the practice jump and then cantered towards her.

"Bad luck in the arena," Daisy said unconvincingly. "I saw you talking to the judges afterwards. What did they want?"

"They told me that I could have another go," Georgie told her. "Since I'd actually gone clear over the wall, technically I'm still in."

"Really?" Daisy said, arching one eyebrow. "You know, I didn't even expect to see you here at all after that crash at Great Brampton. You've got more lives than a cat, Georgie."

"Yeah, I'm thinking of getting myself a collar with a little bell," Georgie said.

Daisy didn't smile. "Well anyway, good luck," she said. "Break a leg."

Georgie couldn't help feeling that Daisy meant it literally. "You too," she replied coolly.

Daisy did an expert show hunter round for the

judges that finished with a display over a full wire fence. Backstage, Georgie watched and waited for the judges' verdict. David McGee and Helen Nicholson both gave her a nine, and then it was Tara's turn.

"I get the impression that these jumps are way below your abilities," Tara said. "I don't think we've witnessed the full extent of your talents here today..." The crowd began to boo but Tara raised a hand to silence them, "...however, I'm impressed by the absolutely perfect position you maintained the entire time. I can see that this Irish Hunter is a challenging mount, but you make him look easy. You ride him beautifully and so..." Tara reached for her score card. "I'm giving you an eight."

The highest score that Tara had given anyone up until that point was a six. An eight was pure gold. Daisy King and Village Voice had the top marks of the day and she was the one to beat.

"I cannot believe they gave her nines!" Georgie heard a snooty girl on a glossy bay complaining as she sat in the wings. It was Felicity Whitfield, renowned for her bad attitude on the show circuit. She had already had her turn in the arena and achieved miserable scores from all the judges. Instead of keeping quiet about it, she had been complaining vigorously about the standards of the judging ever since.

"Have you noticed how Tara is totally into grey horses?" she griped to the girl beside her. "She always favours the greys. She never gives high marks for bays. That's why she only gave me a four!"

The other girl agreed. "We might as well pack up and go home!"

They didn't leave though. Instead, they stayed on the sidelines, whining bitterly and sniping as the other riders took their turns. When the last rider, a boy called Cameron Fraser, entered the ring on a big, coloured cob the girls wasted no time ripping him to pieces.

"Look at the hideous Roman nose on that horse!" Felicity grimaced. "How can he ride a horse with an ugly face like that?"

"I wouldn't be caught dead on it – it looks like a cow!" the other girl opined. "Mind you, he rides as if it's a cow too! Look at his crest release over the jumps!"

"Cameron Fraser is from Coldstream in the Scottish

Border Country," Mike Partridge was telling the crowd. "His coloured cob goes by the show name Sir Galahad, but I understand this horse's nickname is Paddy."

Cameron was dressed in an emerald green hunting jacket that was clearly a hand-me-down. The velvet was faded and the jacket was at least two sizes too big. He was a tall boy for thirteen with pale skin and a thick mop of curly brown hair that poked out from beneath his hard hat. His riding style couldn't have been more different to Daisy King's. He lacked her finesse, but he had raw courage and took the jumps at top speed. He was broadly grinning as he took the last fence. Cameron gave the crowd a cheerful wave before pushing his magnificent black and white horse into a thundering gallop down the long side of the arena. When he finally pulled up to halt in front of the three selectors, Tara Kelly was the first judge to speak. "You're a rough diamond, Cameron," Tara told the boy. "You do everything wrong, but somehow you make it look right. Natural balance and ability in spades... so I'm giving you an eight."

The look on Felicity's face when she heard this was

so funny that Georgie couldn't resist. As she rode past she shouted out to the two girls, "It looks like the judges fancy cows as well as greys!"

With the best scores by far, Daisy and Cameron topped the competition at the end of the day.

"Well, not quite the end," Mike Partridge told the crowd. "Our selectors have asked one of the finalists to perform once more."

In the arena, as he spoke, the crew were busy erecting the puissance jumps.

"Remember our daredevil dual jumpers?" Mike Partridge asked. "Well, we've got one of them back again – Georgie Parker riding Tyro. This time she's jumping alone…" Mike Partridge paused for effect, "and this time the wall is being raised. She's going to try and clear the bricks at a massive one metre sixty-five!"

As the stewards moved the last rows of bricks into place and measured the wall one last time, Georgie stood at the entrance with Lucinda. She took a deep breath and wiped a sweaty palm on her jods. "I'm so nervous!" she told Lucinda. "Have you got any last minute words of advice?"

Lucinda looked at the enormous wall standing in the middle of the arena. "Just three," she said. "Get. Over. It!"

In the ring, Georgie tipped her hat to the selectors and set off on a warm-up lap at a brisk canter. Just like last time, the first jump was the upright rail. Tyro popped over it neatly and then flew the oxer with ease. Now, Georgie turned him to face the wall once more. There was a brief moment when Olivia's gruesome fall flashed through her mind but then Georgie focused on the task at hand. Tyro came in at the jump in a round, collected canter. A couple of metres out from the wall, Georgie felt her stomach clench. What if the black pony failed to lift his feet? What if they struck the wall and crashed? But then Tyro was taking off and they were going up, up and over. She heard his hind legs nudge a brick, but not enough to bring it down and they landed on the other side with the wall still intact. They had done it! They were clear!

"Georgie Parker, ladies and gentlemen," the announcer's voice was turning squeaky with excitement. "How about that – clearing the wall at one metre sixty-five! Well done, Georgie!"

The spotlights were turned on the three judges, ready for their comments. The selectors seemed impressed and were shuffling their score cards. Helen Nicholson was just about to speak when Mike Partridge interrupted.

"I'm sorry, selectors, but it seems the young lady isn't finished," he boomed. "Georgie Parker has asked the jump stewards to raise the wall to the next level, she's attempting another round. The height this time? One metre eighty!"

Georgie rode back into the ring and the crowd was silent. Instead of cantering the pony around to warm up, she took him right up to the jump and let him stand in front of it, just a few metres out from the fence. One metre eighty was a huge height for a pony to jump – and when Tyro stood in front of the wall everyone could see that the jump was taller than he was! How could the gelding conquer this brick barricade when he couldn't even see over it?

"Come on everyone!" Mike Partridge called to the crowd. "They'll never get over it if you don't give them a cheer!"

The crowd burst into applause and shouts of encouragement. It was just the spur that Georgie needed. Suddenly her nerves melted away.

"We're going over it, Tyro," she told her pony. "You and me. We're going over that wall."

As they came around to take the first of the warm-up jumps, Tyro gave a huge buck as if he was too excited about what lay ahead to keep his feet on the ground. Georgie had to check him hard to balance him before the jump, but he cleared the upright easily and cantered on to the oxer. He cleared this too, and gave a buck after the jump. And then another buck!

The bucking didn't faze Georgie. It was Tyro's way of letting her know he was keen and ready to go. As she turned him to face the wall, she could feel her heart thumping in her chest. Then a strange calm came over her and the world seemed to move in slow motion as she urged the pony on and approached the wall.

This was the biggest fence she had ever faced. She couldn't see over to the other side and yet she had faith in her horse. Closer to the jump they came in one stride, two strides and then HUP! Georgie felt Tyro lift off into the air. He was flying now, his feet tucked up at the front, clearing the wall. Could his back legs make it over as well? Tyro flicked up his hind fetlocks like a superstar and the bricks beneath him didn't move. He was over! And the crowd were on their feet cheering. The look on the selectors' faces said it all – a row of beaming smiles. But it was the number on Tara Kelly's card that mattered the most.

"I'm giving you a nine!" she told Georgie.

No matter what happened – no one could take this day away from her. Georgie Parker had won a place at Blainford Academy

Chapter Seven

As Georgie took her victory lap of honour she spotted her dad and Lily in the stands shouting out her name. "Georgie! Over here!" Lily was hard to miss. She was going berserk and trying to start the crowd in a Mexican wave whilst doing wolf whistles. Dr Parker was waving at her and beaming with pride. He had taken his spectacles off to wipe his eyes and looked quite emotional as she cantered by.

It was a bittersweet moment. Georgie and Tyro had done it together. But the last time she had spoken with her father, he had been adamant – there wasn't enough money to take her pony to Blainford.

On the drive home from Birmingham she had given it one more try, begging her dad to find a way to afford Tyro's boarding costs.

"Georgie," Dr Parker sighed, "I wish I could. Believe me, I have really tried. Over the past week I've been through the finances, including our savings. Your mum left enough in a trust to cover the cost of your fees. And I can afford the airfares and your uniforms. But I'm afraid it's simply too expensive for you to take Tyro." Dr Parker paused and then he said in a gentle voice, "I've spoken to the bursar at Blainford and she says they have a school horse available if you want it. It's a much cheaper option. I've talked about this with Lucinda and she said that Blainford school horses are actually quite good..."

"But I don't want to use Blainford horses! I want to take Tyro with me!"

"Georgie!" Her dad was exasperated now. "Don't make this any harder for me. It's just not possible. I'm afraid you're going to have to make a choice. If you really want to go to this school, then you'll have to go alone. Tyro will stay behind."

It was unbearable. Georgie wanted so badly to go to Blainford, but Tyro was her best friend, she couldn't imagine being apart from him. If she couldn't take him with her, then maybe she should give up her place at the academy and stay at home after all.

At the stables the next day, Lucinda put it in perspective for her. "Tyro is a great pony," Lucinda said, "but there'll be other great ponies in your future. And you only get one chance to go to Blainford."

"I don't understand why Dad won't let me take him—" Georgie began, but Lucinda cut her off.

"Blainford is expensive, Georgie. My parents put themselves through all sorts to afford the fees and I had to ride a school horse. I didn't care. I was just grateful for the opportunity – and you should be too."

Lucinda was right. Georgie's dad was already willing to stretch his finances to the limit for her. She was being a brat.

"If I did decide to go," Georgie said, biting her lip and fighting not to cry, "and I left Tyro behind, would you look after him for me?"

Lucinda nodded. "If that's what you want, I can keep Tyro here. I'd love to have him and I could really use him for lessons in the riding school. He'd be a great mount for my more experienced pupils." She paused. "But Tyro is a very talented horse and we have to do what's best for him as well. If you leave him here he's going to get bored pretty fast trotting around the arena with mediocre young riders. Tyro's too good for that. He's an athlete and he needs a competitive home."

"What do you mean?"

"I think you should sell him."

Georgie was horrified. "I'm not selling Tyro!"

"Believe me, I've been in the same position that you're in now many times," Lucinda said kindly. "It's awful, but it comes with the territory. I've had to sell some of my best horses to make ends meet and keep the stable going. It breaks my heart every time, but that's the lot of the competitive rider. If you really want to make it to the top then sometimes you have to let go of horses that are very special to you…" Lucinda looked over at Tyro, "… even the ones that you love."

After she'd mucked out the stables, Georgie stayed late to be with Tyro, grooming him and giving him snuggles. The idea of letting him go seemed unbelievable. But her dad had made the choice quite clear. If she went to Blainford, Tyro wouldn't be coming with her.

✳

"I can't believe you're making so much fuss over a horse!" Lily complained. "What about me? You're quite happy to go away and leave me stuck here in Little Brampton without you!"

The two girls were walking home after school and Lily was back to her usual form. After being thrilled for Georgie about her success at the grand finals she had spent the past week being extremely grouchy at the idea of her best friend moving to the other side of the world.

"You can email me," Georgie countered, "Tyro can't."

Lily kicked a stone beneath her feet. "So when do you leave?" she asked.

"Next term," Georgie said. "The new school year starts at the beginning of September and I'll be in the new intake of first year students."

Lily frowned. "How come you're a first year again?

You'd be in the third year if you stayed in Little Brampton with me."

"It's different over there," Georgie said. "It's a private school. Blainford starts in the eighth grade. You start school as a junior when you're thirteen and then at fifteen you become a senior..."

Lily groaned, "Too complicated! Can we stop talking about this now? My brain hurts."

They had reached the crossroads, where two narrow lanes bordered by hawthorn hedgerows intersected. To the left, the road led down into the village. To the right, the houses were sparse, spread further apart and surrounded by green fields. Lily's house was the closest. It was a pale pink two-storey house, surrounded by rose gardens that Lily's mother tended obsessively. The gardens at Georgie's house got far less attention, but that had been true even when her mother was alive. Mrs Parker had always been far too busy in the stables to bother with the flowerbeds.

The Parker house was a grey stone cottage with a grey slate roof and wrought iron gates. The stables out the back were made from the same grey stone. There were five stalls, and at one time they had all been full of horses, but now they were empty, apart from the odd visit from Bandit, the Parkers' cat, stalking for mice.

Behind the Parkers' property was a bridle path that ran along the river through the woods and connected to the path that led from Lucinda's riding school. The woods were dense, but if you rode far enough you reached open countryside again and wonderful views over the green valleys.

Georgie had never paid much attention to the landscape when she'd hacked out on Tyro in the past, but now that she knew she was leaving, she'd begun noticing just how beautiful it was here. She was developing strange pangs of nostalgia for Little Brampton.

"Really?" Lily had been surprised when Georgie mentioned this. "Name one thing that you'll miss."

"The pies at Thelma's bakery," Georgie told her, "and the cream buns they sell in the school caff. Oh, and baked beans and Marmite – they don't have them in America."

"Have you noticed," Lily said tartly, "that

everything you've listed so far is food?"

The news that Georgie was leaving to go to boarding school in America was the talk of Little Brampton High School. Suddenly everyone was paying her attention. Lily just about hit the roof when she saw that Julie Jenkins, who sat beside Georgie in maths, had actually written the letters BFF inside a giant pink heart on Georgie's maths book!

"Best friends forever?" Lily boggled. "It should say VVA – Very Vague Acquaintance!"

It was weird. Girls that had never bothered to speak to Georgie before were stopping her in the hallways and telling her how much they'd miss her and imploring Georgie to write them emails and keep in touch. How could they miss her, she wondered, when they had barely noticed she was there in the first place?

Georgie was beginning to realise that, apart from Lily and Lucinda and her dad, she wouldn't really miss anyone much in Little Brampton. She had spent her whole life in this village, and yet somehow she had never really felt like she belonged here. It was as if her real life was somewhere else, waiting for her to arrive so that it could finally begin.

For the past week she had stuck her head in the sand about what she was going to do with Tyro. But she knew Lucinda was right. He would be bored at the riding school. And yet she couldn't bear the thought of selling him. Who could possibly understand and love him as much as she did?

She had said her goodbyes to Lily at the crossroads and was walking alone down the lane when the realisation hit her. She raced straight to the phone when she got in. She checked the list of phone numbers in her diary and then dialled, holding her breath and waiting anxiously until someone picked up at the other end. "Hello?" Georgie said. "It's Georgie. I'm phoning because I've made a decision. I'm selling Tyro..." she hesitated, "and I want you to buy him."

✳

Two days later, Georgie stood in Tyro's stall and watched as the sleek grey Range Rover pulled up outside Lucinda's stables. At the sight of the empty horse trailer being towed behind it her hands subconsciously clasped tighter around Tyro's halter. When Olivia and Mrs Prescott stepped out of the Range Rover, Georgie stayed in the stall with Tyro. In the end, Lucinda had to come and get her.

"There you are!" Lucinda gave Georgie a gentle smile. "Have you got him ready?"

Georgie nodded. She'd been at the stables since seven that morning. She'd groomed the black pony for a solid hour, oiling his hooves and pulling his mane. Then she'd dressed him in his best travelling blanket, a lightweight tartan rug, and Velcroed on his padded floating boots so that he was all ready to be loaded on to the trailer.

Tyro had been to so many horse shows he knew what this routine meant. He was dressed to go somewhere and now he had an air of anticipation about him. What he didn't know was that this time there was no show. He would be taking this trip without Georgie and he would not be returning.

"You'd probably hate it in Lexington, anyway," Georgie told the black pony as she brushed his pretty face, smoothing down his long forelock. "All the horses will have American accents!"

Tyro nickered as if he had got the joke and nudged Georgie with his muzzle, looking for carrots in her pockets. They had their own ways of communicating, she and Tyro. In three years, their bond had become so strong.

"Come on," Lucinda said gently, "leave him here for a moment and say hi to Olivia and her mum."

When Georgie had phoned Olivia two days ago and offered to sell her the black Connemara, Olivia couldn't quite believe her luck. Now that Molly needed complete rest until next season, she had been left high and dry without a competition horse. Tyro was the perfect solution.

"Of course I want to buy him!" Olivia told Georgie. "But are you sure you want to sell him?"

Georgie steeled herself and tried to be strong. "Yes, I'm sure," she said. She didn't want to sell Tyro, of course, but it really was the best thing to do. He deserved to have a proper life with an owner who loved him. And she couldn't think of anyone better to sell her beloved pony to than Olivia.

Olivia was totally aware of how hard this decision must have been for Georgie. And so, when she arrived with her mother at the stables that morning, she wasn't expecting the usual cheerful greeting from her friend. When Georgie did finally emerge from the stables, Olivia took one look at her miserable face and rushed up and gave her a huge hug.

"I've got the same stall ready for him at my house," she told Georgie. "The one that he stayed in when we were training for the final auditions. He'll feel at home straight away. I've told Molly he's coming too – she's going to love having a paddock mate."

Georgie handed Olivia a piece of paper. "I wrote down everything I could think of, you know, little things that you need to know." She managed a weak smile. "He likes peppermints. I give them as a treat after training sometimes. And he loves molasses in his hard feed... he's quite a greedy eater..."

Olivia listened as Georgie ran through the list of do's and don'ts. Then Lucinda emerged from the stables leading Tyro and Georgie felt her heart sink. This was really it then. This was goodbye.

"Do you want to be the one to load him on to the trailer, Georgie?" Mrs Prescott asked.

Georgie took the lead rope with a trembling hand and walked Tyro down the driveway as Olivia and Mrs Prescott dropped the ramp of the trailer. Then she circled Tyro back and walked him up the ramp. The black pony always loaded perfectly and he followed behind her into the trailer and stood calmly as the ramp was raised behind him.

A few minutes later, when Georgie still hadn't emerged out of the trailer, Mrs Prescott began to worry and stuck her head in the front door. "Is everything OK in there? Are you having trouble doing up the rope?" she asked. "There's a steel hook at the back of the hay net to tie him up."

"I'm OK," Georgie replied. She had already tied Tyro up. But she couldn't come back out of the horse trailer just yet as she needed to stop crying. Taking a deep breath and drying her eyes one last time, she buried her face in Tyro's mane and hugged the pony hard with her hands tight around his neck.

"Don't forget me," she told the pony breathlessly. "I promise, I won't forget you."

Despite Georgie's efforts to pull herself together, when she emerged from the trailer everyone could see how upset she was. Mrs Prescott realised that the best thing to do was leave straight away. So Olivia gave Georgie another hasty hug and jumped into the passenger seat. Mrs Prescott shook hands with Lucinda and then came over to Georgie, said goodbye and pressed a folded-over piece of paper into her hand.

Georgie watched with tears rolling down her cheeks as the Range Rover and the trailer towing Tyro headed down the driveway, past the crumbling stone walls of the riding school, disappearing from sight behind the overgrown hawthorn hedgerows. Then she remembered the piece of paper that Mrs Prescott had handed to her and opened it up. It was a cheque for twenty thousand pounds.

✳

Dr Parker was stunned when Georgie came home and presented him with the cheque. He had been shocked enough when his daughter told him she was selling the pony, and was even more so when he discovered just how much the Connemara was worth.

"You can put it towards my fees at Blainford," Georgie told her father. But he shook his head. "Your fees have been paid – for this year at least," he told her. "You keep the money. We'll bank it as a pony fund for the future. I'm sure you'll want to buy a new horse one day."

It had been hard saying goodbye to Tyro, but in the end it was much worse saying goodbye to Lily. Her best friend was in floods of tears as she hugged her at the airport and thrust a last minute present into her hands. It was wrapped in pretty lilac paper with an enormous gold bow.

"Can I open it now?" Georgie asked.

Lily sniffled and nodded. Georgie tore the paper open to reveal… a jar of Marmite.

"You said they didn't have it in America," Lily giggled.

"Thank you!" Georgie gave her a massive hug. "Whenever I eat toast I shall think of you!"

Lucinda had already given her a gift before they left

Little Brampton. It was a new back protector and the note that was attached read: "Wear this for Tara Kelly's class – no broken bones for you!"

"Thanks, Lucinda!" Georgie had been thrilled with her gift.

"You're the second generation of Parker women to attend Blainford Academy," Lucinda told her. "I'm very proud of you – and your mother would have been proud too."

Georgie had wiped away the tears as Lucinda said this. It had been Ginny Parker's dream that her daughter would follow in her footsteps and go to Blainford. And now, here Georgie was, about to board the plane!

Her dad tried so hard, but he didn't have a clue really. At the airport shop he had bought her books for the plane. "The lady behind the counter said you'd be bound to like these," he said hopefully as he passed them over. Georgie could tell straight away by the pink sparkly covers that she would not like them at all. But she smiled and took them anyway. She didn't want to disappoint her dad.

At the check-in counter she was feeling all jet set and sophisticated about travelling alone – until the stewardess put a huge red sticker on her bag with the letters UM on it: Unaccompanied Minor. Then she put a great big UM sticker on Georgie's jumper too!

"There's going to be a driver from Blainford to meet you at the other end," Georgie's dad told her. He looked tense and worried at the airport gates and when he hugged her goodbye Georgie thought he wasn't going to let her go. "Call me when you arrive and let me know that you made it safely," Dr Parker said as he waved her off.

"I will," she promised.

As she boarded the plane, Georgie thought she would feel scared or homesick. But from the moment the engines revved and the plane took off she felt her heart soaring along with it. She would miss Little Brampton, but a part of her couldn't wait to leave. As the plane rose up in the sky she felt her old life falling away. She was leaving it behind and starting again. At Blainford, she could be herself at last. She could be anyone she wanted to be.

Chapter Eight

*T*hey call Lexington 'bluegrass country' but the grass wasn't actually blue. It was deep, verdant green. "The best horse country in the world," Kenny told Georgie as he loaded her bags into his car. Kenny was Blainford Academy's driver. He had been standing at the airport gates holding a sign with Georgie's name on it when she got off the plane. Kenny wore a blue baseball cap that said *Wildcats* on the front in gold letters and he chewed tobacco constantly, which made it even harder to understand his thick Southern accent.

"This here road we're on now is called Man O' War Boulevard," Kenny told Georgie as they pulled away from the airport terminal. "You heard of Man O' War, right?" Georgie had to admit that she hadn't and Kenny shook his head in amazement. "You mean to say you're here to go to this fancy horse school and you don't know who Man O' War was?" Kenny laughed. "He was one of the greatest racehorses of all time."

Georgie looked out the window. They had turned left now on to the main highway, signposted with the word 'Versailles'. *Ver-sigh*. That was how Kenny pronounced it in his Kentucky drawl. The countryside was so big and open compared to the dinky fields and hawthorn hedges of Little Brampton. Pristine white plank fencelines ran for mile after mile, bordering the lush green pastures. Tall trees lined the long driveways which led to magnificent sprawling mansions. As the fields flashed past, Georgie saw elegant Thoroughbred mares grazing with their leggy young offspring at foot.

"Are there a lot of racehorse farms around here?" she asked.

Kenny snorted as if this were a joke. "Nearly five hundred in this district alone." He pointed at a stately white mansion surrounded by red and white barns with green rooftops. "That one there is Calumet Farm.

114

One of the greatest racehorse studs in Kentucky, home to Triple Crown winner, Citation."

"I'm not really into racehorses," Georgie said, "I ride eventers."

Kenny scratched his head. "Eventers, huh? Yeah, we got those here in Lexington too. Can't say they interest me much – I'm a betting man. I like being trackside on that first Saturday in May. My idea of a perfect horse is the one that crosses the Derby finish line first with my money on his back."

They were almost on the outskirts of Versailles. "Not much further now," he told Georgie and she felt her stomach tense up.

Eight hours from London to New York. Another two hours at the terminal and then a two-hour connecting flight from New York to Lexington. It had taken forever to get here and now suddenly the moment of arrival was looming too quickly. She wasn't ready to be at Blainford yet – all on her own at a strange school where she didn't know anyone.

The signpost ahead said it was only three more miles to Versailles, but Kenny turned off the main highway and headed down a back road, before turning the car again into a private lane. "This is it," he told her. "Blainford Academy."

In front of them were two enormous pale-blue wrought iron gates with the Blainford insignia worked into the pattern of filigreed metal. Kenny pressed a button on the intercom and the gates swung open automatically. He drove through, steering the car down a broad avenue shaded by oak trees on either side. The plank fences here were stained black instead of the usual Kentucky white, and Georgie could see a strange assortment of horse breeds grazing in the fields. There was a striking chocolate-brown Appaloosa, with a white blanket of spots on his rump. Grazing happily alongside him was a jet-black horse, which she recognised as Friesian with its long flowing mane, glossy coat and 'feathers' of long silky hair on his legs. Those two rare breeds side by side were unusual enough, but there were others.

"Ohmygod!" Georgie's eyes widened when she saw the most incredible horse, as fine-boned and sleek as a greyhound. She could tell immediately by the wide-set intelligent eyes and dished face that this was a purebred Arab. Yet it was big for an Arabian, almost sixteen hands with a coat of burnished chestnut that sparkled in the Kentucky sunshine.

Georgie was certain she also saw a Haflinger, a stocky Austrian breed, a heavy-set pony with a trademark golden coat and milky white, silky mane and tail. There was a beautiful palomino, with the sturdy rump and proportions of a Western Quarterhorse, and next to it, a haughty-looking grey that was so ghostly pale it was almost white. It had a thick crest and a Roman nose. Was it a Lipizzaner? One of the dancing horses of the Spanish Riding School? It had to be! Her heart was racing with excitement. She had never seen so many breeds all together at once in her life!

"Whose horses are they?" she asked Kenny.

Kenny shrugged as if the rare breeds were nothing special at all. "That's school grazing. Those horses belong to the students," he replied.

They were approaching the curve at the end of the oak driveway, and finally the school itself came into view. Georgie had seen the photos in the prospectus, but here in front of her was the real Blainford – and it was glorious. The main building rose up two storeys high, a grand old antebellum Georgian mansion made of red brick with columns out the front, white-trimmed dormer windows on the second floor and three turret rooms that jutted up into the sky out of the red shingled roofline. A vast stone archway in the front of the building led into a courtyard where a large square lawn was bordered by broad footpaths and red brick buildings on every side. Cars could drive through here and Kenny steered the car under the archway to a parking bay immediately on the right. He stopped there, got out and unloaded Georgie's suitcases.

"Someone will come for your luggage. I'll go to the office and let Mrs Dubois know that you've arrived," he said.

He strode off across the lawn leaving Georgie standing beside her suitcases, trying not to feel self-conscious. A few of the students wandering about the courtyard were staring at her. Even though school didn't officially begin for another day yet, pupils had already been returning after their holidays. Georgie was beginning to regret arriving in her own clothes. She had decided on a T-shirt and jeans as she hadn't wanted to wear the school uniform on the plane. But now she felt badly out of place. Everyone else was dressed in regulation Blainford uniforms. The girls wore either a pale blue pinafore dress, or a pale blue shirt with navy jodhpurs. The boys were in a navy shirt and black jods. The fact that she hadn't had a shower and probably had bad slept-on-an-aeroplane hair wasn't helping her feel any better. She wished Kenny would hurry back with Mrs Dubois – whoever she was.

Georgie looked across the lawn. Kenny had disappeared into a building on the other side of the square. Perhaps he had meant for her to follow him? She began to stride out across the grass courtyard heading in the same direction.

"Hey!" a stern voice barked. She turned around and saw a boy, three or four years older than her, walking towards her.

"No walking on the quad," the boy said. He was freckle-faced with russet-coloured hair and a confident set to his jawline. He wore long black boots and spurs, which indicated his senior status at the school. Juniors were only allowed to wear short brown jodhpur boots.

"What?" Georgie didn't understand.

"You're standing on the quad," the boy said again as if she were an idiot. "That'll earn you a fatigue."

"I'm really sorry, but I don't know what you're talking about," Georgie said.

"The quad," the boy said slowly, as if he were talking to a small child, "...is this green piece of lawn. You're not allowed on it. I'm giving you a fatigue."

"But you're standing on it," Georgie frowned.

"Prefects are allowed on the quad," the boy replied. Georgie realised now that they weren't alone. A group of students were standing under the eaves of the building that Georgie had been making her way towards. They were watching and sniggering.

"Come on, Conrad," one of the boys called out. "Leave her alone. She's obviously new."

"No excuse," Conrad shot back. "First years need to learn the rules."

The one who had called out to Conrad came over

towards them now. He was wearing short boots, but he looked too old to be a first year. His navy school shirt and black jodhpurs were rumpled and worn and he had messy blond hair and a tan like a surfer.

"They should never have given you prefect's spurs, Conrad," the blond boy groaned. "Power has corrupted you. You're out of control."

Conrad clearly didn't find this funny. "You're only a second year, James, you shouldn't be on the quad either. Get off the grass or I'll give you fatigues as well."

Conrad didn't bother to look at the other boy as he said this. He kept his eyes on Georgie. His stare was beginning to unnerve her. "What's your name?"

"Georgie Parker."

"You're on fatigues, Parker. And get off the quad right now!" He turned his back on her and began to walk away. "Come on, James," he said, clearly expecting the blond boy to follow him.

James shrugged and gave Georgie a smile. She noticed the cute way that his mouth went crooked when he grinned. "I'm sorry about Conrad," he said. "What can I say? He fell off without his hard hat last term and he hasn't been the same since..."

"Now, James!" Conrad was stalking off across the quad.

"See you later, Parker." James gave her another lopsided smile and walked off, just as Kenny and a solidly-built woman with a swept-back bouffant of blue-grey hair finally emerged from the building.

Georgie still didn't really understand what had just happened. She didn't even know what a 'fatigue' was. She certainly knew that she disliked Conrad but the other boy, James, was different. There was an easy charm about him with his blue eyes and unkempt hair. When he smiled that crooked grin, he was outrageously cute.

"I'm Mrs Dubois, the school bursar. I'm very sorry to keep you waiting, Miss Parker," the woman said as she reached Georgie's side. "However, in future please make sure you don't stand on the quad." She gestured to the grass square. "Only prefects and school masters are allowed to walk on it."

"I just found that out," Georgie said.

"Now," Mrs Dubois continued, "normally I would give you a tour of the school and show you the junior dorms and stables, but I have several other new arrivals turning up shortly and I really can't leave the office. So I'll ask one of the girls to show you around instead…"

Mrs Dubois's eyes scanned the courtyard looking for a suitable candidate.

"Hey there, Mrs Dubois!" A girl with glossy black hair cut in a short blunt bob had appeared out of nowhere and was standing eagerly beside them. Mrs Dubois leapt back.

"Alice!" she said looking flustered. "Don't creep up on people!"

"Do you need some help, Mrs Dubois?" Alice asked sweetly. "Do you want me to show her around?"

Mrs Dubois looked very doubtful. Once again she cast her eyes around the quad, clearly hoping a better candidate might present themselves. Alice continued to stand there, smiling as if butter wouldn't melt in her mouth.

"All right, Alice," Mrs Dubois sighed. She turned to Georgie. "This is Alice Dupree. Alice – this is Georgina Parker. She's in Badminton House and she's got a horse in stable block C."

"Don't worry—I'll give her a real tour. See you later, Mrs Dubois," Alice sing-songed as the bursar walked back towards her office. As soon as she was out of earshot, Alice's saccharine smile disappeared.

"Man, she is so uptight!" she groaned. "Did you see the look she gave me?"

"I saw it," Georgie nodded. "She thinks you're trouble."

Alice Dupree gave a thoughtful chew of the bubblegum in her mouth and the gum made a loud crack as it snapped. "She's probably right!" she said gleefully.

✳

Alice Dupree didn't seem very interested in her role as tour guide. She mostly wanted to gossip.

"What was Conrad Miller saying to you?" Alice hissed conspiratorially.

"He was telling me off for walking on the grass," Georgie said. "At least I think that was what he was doing. It was a bit confusing."

"That guy is such a polo poseur. I can't stand him."

Alice snapped her gum again. Then she stared hard at Georgie. "You're not going to go polo on me are you?" she asked.

"What do you mean?" Georgie knew she was tired from the flight, but she was getting fed up with this. Ever since she'd arrived, people kept asking her questions she didn't understand.

Alice blew a bubble and waited for it to pop before she spoke again. "What sort of rider are you? What's your major?"

"I thought we didn't have to choose a major subject until we became seniors?" Georgie said.

Alice nodded. "Well, yeah, that's true. But even the juniors get to choose their option subjects. Besides, at Blainford your major isn't just about how you ride, it's who you are." She entwined her arm in Georgie's and walked beside her so that she could talk in a confidential whisper.

"You know, like Conrad and his crew. They're the polo boys. A very exclusive little club – you have to be rich and a total jerk to join them. Or..." Alice said, "if you're a girl you can always hang out with the showjumperettes instead." She rolled her eyes as she said this.

"So showjumperettes are…"

"The worst! Total trust fund brats!" Alice said emphatically. "Mind you, at least they're not all hippie and drippy like the natural horsemanship losers, or totally into line dancing to Miley Cyrus like the Western riders…" Alice groaned, "…and do not even get me started on how uncool it is to hang out with the dressage geeks."

Georgie frowned. "How do you know I'm not one of them? A dressage geek, I mean…"

Alice laughed. "For a start, dressage geeks are usually German or Dutch. They're OK but they're not exactly wildcats, if you know what I mean. No, you're not a dressage geek. I'm a pretty good judge of these things. I'm guessing you're an eventing major – just like me. Am I right?"

Georgie nodded. "Yeah, actually."

"I knew it!" Alice shrieked and pulled Georgie closer. "You and I are gonna be best friends."

Alice had been so busy talking that it took Georgie a

moment to realise they'd walked all the way through the quad and were out the other side. They hadn't even taken a look at the classrooms.

"Oh yeah. I forgot about the tour," Alice said when Georgie pointed this out. She looked back at the block of buildings. "Lemme see," she said, peering into the distance and pointing vaguely in the direction of the school. "You see that room on the end there? That's biology, and that one beside it is English." She perked up as she said this, as if a thought had occurred to her, "You should be good at English because you're, like, from England right?"

"Uh… I guess so." Georgie was baffled by this logic but Alice barely paused for breath before she continued, "That's French class on the top floor. The first year home room is somewhere at the front of the building on the first floor and… I don't have a clue where anything else is."

Alice grinned. "That'll do for the boring tour."

Still walking arm-in-arm Alice steered Georgie away from the main school along one of the many bridle paths that criss-crossed the grounds. "You're allowed to ride your horse everywhere – except the quad obviously, and you can't take them to the classrooms off the quad either," Alice continued. "All the dull school stuff like maths and history happens over there in the morning. Then after lunch the horse classes begin."

"You seem to know your way around the place," Georgie said.

"Both my sisters are Blainford girls," Alice told her, "I know everything about this place – and everyone in it!"

"Do your sisters still go here?" Georgie asked.

"Cherry left school last year so she's back on our family's farm in Maryland. She's riding the showjumping circuit this season," Alice said. "My other sister Kendal is still here – she's in her final senior year. She's nice but she can go a bit polo sometimes. She actually used to go out with that creep Conrad!" Alice pulled a face and then yanked Georgie by the arm down the path to the right.

"Badminton House is over there." Alice pointed to the left where a pathway led past more stables and a duck pond. "We can go there later. Let's go to the stables first and see if we can find your horse!"

Georgie wondered how Alice would react when she told her she was riding one of the school's horses. But Alice was unfazed. "Some of the kids here are snobby about that stuff," she admitted. "The showjumperettes totally judge you by the horse you ride. They're always trying to outdo each other with their Selle Francais and fancy Warmbloods. But I don't care."

"So what's your horse like?" Georgie asked.

"Actually, he's a fancy Warmblood," Alice giggled. "His show name is William the Conqueror and his full brother just won the horse trials at Burghley."

"Wow!" Georgie was impressed. But Alice acted like this was no big deal.

"Will's a sweetheart. He used to belong to Kendal so he's a hand-me-down horse. This is my first season on him."

Alice strolled into the stables as if she had been here all her life. She skipped between the solid wooden sliding doors and into the dark cavernous interior.

"Your name should already be on the wall," she told Georgie. "Usually they have a list up saying which horse the school has assigned you... here it is!"

There was a blackboard list of riders' names and beside each, written in pastel chalk, was the name of their horse.

Georgie scanned the list to find her name. Standing beside her, Alice was doing the same thing.

"There's your name!" Alice said. "Georgina Parker. You've been assigned to ride... Belladonna. Stall seven."

"Belladonna," Georgie said, trying the name out, seeing how it sounded. This was the horse that she would ride for the rest of the year at Blainford. She had spent the past weeks lost in daydreams, wondering what her new horse would be like. She felt nervous about meeting the horse for the first time. Alice, however, wasn't one to hesitate.

"Let's go!" Alice was already off and racing down the corridor towards the loose boxes. "The horses' names and numbers are on their stalls. You check the ones on the right," she shouted back at Georgie, "I'll do the other side."

They began working their way down the stables, Alice on the left hand side and Georgie checking the right. When Alice called out, "I've found her!" Georgie's feet barely even touched the ground as she raced across the corridor to join her.

The loose boxes in the stable blocks at Blainford were fitted with classic Dutch doors that opened in two halves so that you could shut the bottom and leave the top door open for the horse to stick their head out. Right now, both the top door and bottom door of the stall beside Alice were firmly bolted shut. The nameplate on the door was engraved brass. It said: BELLADONNA

Alice looked at Georgie "Do you want me to open it?"

"No," Georgie said. "It's OK. I can do it."

She reached her hand up and slid the bolt gently open, swinging back the wooden door so that she could see into the loose box.

She heard a gentle nicker and then a moment later a horse emerged into the sunlight. She was a strikingly beautiful mare, a deep red bay with a jet-black mane and tail and a face that had an exquisite sculptural quality to it, as if an ancient Greek had chiselled it from marble. On her forehead was a heart-shaped white marking. Georgie took one look at her and reeled back, as if she had been given an electric shock.

"Georgie? What's wrong?" Alice asked.

Georgie didn't answer. She just stared wide-eyed at the bay mare.

"I think she's beautiful," Alice said. "What's the matter? Don't you like her?"

Georgie shook her head. "No... I mean, it's not that. It's just that I know her already. I know this horse."

Georgie stared, taking in the white heart marking on her forehead, the deep brown eyes. In every way, this horse was the spitting image of Boudicca. She remembered that mare's face so clearly. How could she possibly forget? Boudicca was the horse that her mother had been riding at Blenheim. The day that she died.

Chapter Nine

"You're Ginny Parker's daughter?" Alice was stunned. "*The* Ginny Parker? And you think this is your mother's horse?"

Georgie nodded. "It could be her, I suppose. Dad sold all the horses after the accident. I never found out what happened to Boudicca. I guess she could have been sold to Blainford."

Was it really possible that the mare had somehow ended up here? Georgie had never seen Boudicca again after the day of the accident. Her father had been so upset he wouldn't have the horse back in their stables and she had been sold at auction straight away. Boudicca had been Ginny Parker's favourite horse, but had also been her most difficult mount. Young and headstrong, the bay mare had been the one horse in her stables that Ginny would never let her daughter ride.

Georgie needed a step-ladder to climb on to Ivanhoe, her mum's seventeen hands Irish Hunter, but she had been allowed to ride him over jumps all the same. But not Boudicca.

"She's a sensitive mare, very highly strung," Ginny had said firmly one day when Georgie begged to try out the mare. "You're not ready for a horse like that yet."

The mare in the stall was unnervingly similar to her mother's old horse but the nameplate didn't say Boudicca – it said Belladonna. Whether this mare was Boudicca or not, Georgie was spooked by the resemblance.

"If you don't want to ride her, you could ask Tara Kelly to swap you to a different horse," Alice told her.

"Tara Kelly?"

"She's responsible for matching the school horses up with new riders," Alice explained.

Georgie stared over the Dutch door nervously. Inside her stall, Belladonna was pacing about warily, as if she too was unsettled by her new partnership. The mare's dark eyes were blazing. Georgie wasn't certain what to make of this horse. All she knew was that when Alice suggested that Georgie should come and meet William, she agreed a little too quickly, locking Belladonna's stable door with unnatural haste.

William was just a few doors down in the same stable block. He was a handsome chestnut Warmblood with a broad white stripe down his nose and white spots across his shoulders and rump, a bit like Zara Phillips' famous eventing mount, Toytown.

"He's gorgeous," Georgie enthused as William thrust his nose out of the stall to greet them.

Alice glowed with pride. "He is a lovely boy, isn't he? Will's fifteen years old now. Kendal had him for his best years, but he still has plenty of gas in the tank. He's brilliant on the cross-country course."

They left the stables and walked in a loop around the back of the school and the duck pond, past two of the other boarding houses Alice identified as Luhmuhlen and Alberta.

"There are six houses at the school and each of them

is named after a famous eventing horse trial. The boys' boarding houses are Burghley, Lexington and Luhmuhlen. The girls' houses are Alberta, Badminton and Stars of Pau. Badminton is the best one to be in," Alice insisted.

Badminton House reminded Georgie of a Southern Belle's ball gown. It was a pale blue wooden two-storey building with ribbons of scarlet trim around the upstairs dormer windows and a bright scarlet front door.

Inside, the house had the same Southern charm. Downstairs there was a living room with sofas and a giant television, a kitchen and a bathroom block. There were enough showers and mirrors so the forty girls who lived here wouldn't be fighting for space in the mornings. A huge wooden staircase led upstairs to the senior girls' bedrooms.

"Kendal is a senior so she gets her own room upstairs," Alice said. The junior bedrooms were downstairs and the girls slept two to a room. The room mates were rotated each term. Mrs Birdwell, the house mistress, had already allocated their rooms for the first term. Alice eagerly checked the whiteboard to see who they were sharing with. She frowned. "I'm in with some girl called Emily Tait," she said, "and you're supposed to be rooming with Daisy King." Georgie let out a groan.

"Do you know her?"

"I used to ride against her back in England," Georgie told Alice. "I don't think she likes me much. She's certainly not going to be thrilled when she discovers that she's come all the way to Lexington to room with me."

There was a devious glint in Alice's eyes. "What if she never finds out?"

Alice looked around hastily to see if anyone was watching and then she grabbed the whiteboard eraser. In a moment the deed was done. She had swapped the names over so that Daisy King was now rooming with Emily Tait and Alice and Georgie's names were side by side.

"I cannot believe you just did that!" Georgie was shocked.

"No need to thank me," Alice grinned. "Just let me

have the bed by the window."

All the bedrooms were decorated with floral curtains and duvets in similar patterns but with different colour schemes. Georgie and Alice's had a blue theme, which Georgie faintly registered as she collapsed on top of her duvet. Jetlag from the long flight had struck at last. She was suddenly utterly exhausted and fell asleep then and there, face down on her duvet.

Anyone who has ever flown on a long-distance plane flight will know what jetlag feels like. It is the most uncontrollable phenomenon, where waves of tiredness can appear from out of nowhere. When Alice tried to rouse Georgie half an hour later to go to the dining hall with the other girls Georgie murmured that she was too tired. Alice left her in their room and promised to try to smuggle something back for her to eat later.

When the girls returned from dinner, they found Georgie still sprawled face down on her duvet, sound asleep. No one saw any point in trying to wake her until morning.

✳

The next morning Georgie dressed for the first time in her Blainford pale blue pinafore and navy jersey and sandals, an outfit Alice referred to as 'number ones'. Number twos meant the jodhpurs, shirt and boots that were worn for the riding classes in the afternoons.

"How's the jetlag?" Alice asked as Georgie returned from the bathroom.

"I woke up at five this morning and couldn't get back to sleep," Georgie groaned. "And I'm starving!"

Boarding students ate their meals at the dining hall next to the quad in the main school buildings and it was a five-minute walk up the driveway at the front of the school to get there.

An early morning mist had settled over the school as Alice and Georgie joined the rest of the Badminton girls gathering outside the boarding house. Kendal, Alice's older sister, was standing with the seniors. Georgie would never have recognised her if Alice hadn't pointed her out. The sisters looked nothing alike. Kendal was blonde and tanned, not dark haired like Alice.

"Georgie!" Daisy King waved and came over.

"Wow!" Daisy said. "Amazing, huh? I never thought you and I would both be at Blainford together."

It was hard to tell what she meant by this. Was she amazed that they were here together – or amazed that Georgie had got into Blainford at all?

"So has your horse arrived yet?" Daisy asked.

Georgie shook her head. "I sold Tyro," she said, "I'm going to be riding a school horse."

"Oh, me too!" the girl standing next to Daisy exclaimed. She turned out to be Daisy's room mate, Emily Tait. Emily had an accent, which Georgie had assumed was Australian until Emily said it was "too expensive to fly my horse over from New Zealand".

"It can't be that much more than flying your horse from England," Daisy said dismissively. "I wouldn't have dreamed of coming without Village Voice."

Daisy and Emily seemed distinctly uncomfortable together. Emily, who was shy and quiet, was obviously a bit daunted by her confident, competitive room mate. She hardly said a word after that as they walked up the driveway and Daisy looked like she could barely be bothered talking to her.

"Look at them!" Alice elbowed Georgie. "They're getting on like a house on fire," she said dryly. "They'll thank us one day for putting them together!"

Alice did enough talking for everyone as they walked up the driveway. "Badminton is the best girls' house to be in," she raved. "It's one of the first houses, it was the original girls' boarding house when the school opened and there's always a cool mix of international students." Alice pointed to a stark, white modern-looking building at the point where the driveway forked. "That's Alberta House. The showjumperettes are always in Alberta."

The best boys' house to be in, according to Alice, was Burghley, "because it's the closest one to the school and the stables. You have to walk for miles if you're in Lexington or Luhmuhlen."

Burghley House stood right beside the driveway only a hundred metres from the main school. It was a red Georgian brick building surrounded by rhododendrons and magnolias in bloom. As they walked past, a group of boys came out the front door and Georgie's heart skipped a beat. There was James, the handsome blond boy she had met on the square yesterday. He was walking with the other two boys who had stood back and sniggered when she was being given fatigues.

Georgie glanced across at them and saw the blond boy staring at her. He gave her that same killer smile and she felt her cheeks go hot with embarrassment and hastily turned away to talk to Alice.

This time when they reached the quad Georgie knew better than to walk across the lawn. The girls made their way to the door of the dining hall. They had arrived ahead of the boys from Burghley House, but as they queued at the dining room door, Conrad and two other boys in long boots and spurs pushed straight past them to the front of the line.

"Hey!" Alice snapped. "There's a queue you know!"

Conrad glared at her. "Not for prefects there isn't," he said dismissively, grabbing a breakfast tray from the stack and entering the hall.

The queue moved slowly and by the time the girls finally got inside it was well past eight. Most of the tables were almost full, but there was some space at the far end of the hall where three girls sat. Georgie loaded up her tray with toast, juice and cereal and was about to walk over to join them when Alice blocked her with her breakfast tray.

"No way!" she hissed. "You can't sit over there with them!"

"Why not?" Georgie was baffled.

"That's the showjumperettes' table," Alice said, steering Georgie in the opposite direction where another table had now become free. "And those three girls are the Blainford equivalent to the witches in *Macbeth*."

Alice tried to look like she wasn't staring at the three girls as she pointed them out to Georgie. "The one on the end with the long blonde hair? That's Tori Forsythe, she's a total snob. The girl next to her with the dark hair who looks like she spent all day at the beauty parlour? That's Arden Mortimer. Her parents own, like, half the corn in Iowa. She's a trust fund brat." Alice looked over at Arden who was studiously filing her bright lilac painted fingernails instead of eating her breakfast. "Apparently she got kicked out of her last prep school

143

and her parents threatened to send her to finishing school in Switzerland, but they compromised and sent her here instead."

The third girl had long glossy red hair and was very pretty, with bright green eyes and a deep expensive-looking tan. She had the same pinafore on as Georgie and the others, but it looked so much better on her! She had altered the hemline so that instead of sagging down to the knees like Georgie's did, her uniform sat at a flirty mid-thigh length that showed off her tanned, toned legs.

"Kennedy Kirkwood," Alice said. "She's from Maryland, like me. I competed against her in the US final auditions."

"She's not a senior?" Georgie was surprised.

"She acts like she is," Alice agreed, "but she's only in our year. She's behaving like she owns the school already..." Alice ate another mouthful of cereal and then added, "...although she kinda does. The Kirkwoods donated a new school gymnasium last year. They're super-rich. They have this amazing equestrian estate. Kennedy will probably go home most weekends to ride."

144

"How?" Georgie was puzzled. "It would take her all weekend just to drive home."

Alice laughed. "Who said anything about driving? The Kirkwoods pick the kids up in one of their private jets."

"One of their jets?"

"They've got two. Kennedy goes to Paris each season to get new jodhpurs, and flies her showjumping instructor, Hans Schockelmann, over from Germany so he can give her lessons," Alice continued. "I mean, don't get me wrong. I don't hate her because she's rich. There are other reasons to hate her."

"You sound like you know her pretty well," Georgie said.

"Kennedy and I were best friends at pony club in Maryland – until I beat her in a big competition," Alice admitted. "She demanded that the judges drug test my horse."

"That sounds bad," Georgie said.

"We were only six years old at the time!" Alice laughed.

"You're kidding!"

"Totally serious!" Alice was wide-eyed. "We were just little kids on tiny ponies but for Kennedy it was as if we were at the Olympics. She's always been that way. She can't stand to lose at anything. She hardly speaks to me now."

Georgie's eyes were still fixed on the showjumperettes' table and she was surprised when she saw James suddenly appear at Kennedy's side. He had been walking with his friends towards the exit, but then he diverted course and stopped at their table instead. He said something to Kennedy and the red-haired girl looked up at him and smiled. Then, to Georgie's utter mortification, they both looked over in her direction! James was staring straight at her as he spoke this time and Kennedy was looking at her and laughing.

Georgie hastily looked away and pretended to eat her breakfast, but out of the corner of her eye she could still see Kennedy and James together. Kennedy was chatting and waving her hands about in an animated fashion while the blond boy listened, smiling at her indulgently. Then finally, he said his goodbyes and headed for the door where his friends were waiting for him.

"Are we actually supposed to eat this?" Daisy asked.

"Mmmph? What?" Georgie replied absentmindedly.

"This toast." Daisy was inspecting the slice on her plate. It had the consistency of cardboard. "I mean, is it actually supposed to be edible?"

Alice shrugged and bit into her toast without fear. "Get used to it. Boarding school food is the worst!"

"Hi!" a voice beside them interrupted. "Can I sit with you?" The girls turned round. There was a boy standing by their table holding a breakfast tray. He had short brown hair, brown eyes and an eager grin that made him kind of good-looking, in a geeky way.

"I thought it was you," he smiled. "It's Georgie Parker, isn't it?" The boy had a lilting Scottish accent.

Georgie looked blankly at him. "Yeah, that's me..."

The boy looked a little upset that Georgie clearly didn't recognise him. "It's the hair," he sighed. "My mum cut it before I left. She said she didn't want me going off to Blainford looking like I had a floor mop on my head."

He looked over at Daisy and gave her a smile. "Hey there, Daisy!"

"Hi, Cameron," Daisy smiled back. Georgie looked at the boy again and suddenly she clicked. Cameron Fraser, from the final auditions in Birmingham!

"I remember now," Georgie said as the boy sat down at the table with them. "I didn't recognise you without that big piebald cob. Is he with you?"

"Paddy?" Cameron asked. "Oh yeah, he's with me. He's just gone back for a second helping of scrambled eggs."

Georgie groaned. "I meant have you brought him to school."

"Yeah, he's here," Cameron said, "although he's nearly been kicked out of Blainford already for his behaviour. He managed to jump out of his field last night and eat the middle of the flowerbed at the front of the school gates. He completely devoured the horse shoe from the school insignia. Mrs Dubois had a fit when she saw it."

Georgie giggled. "Bad Paddy."

"Actually, that's pretty typical behaviour for Paddy," Cameron admitted. "He was a champion show horse until he got his leg stuck in a metal gate. The wounds healed but the scars meant he couldn't be shown any more so he got sold on to the local hunt master. He was such a lunatic on the hunting field no one would ride him. Then my mum and dad turned up and offered a hundred quid for him."

"Why did your parents buy him if he was so crazy?" Alice asked.

"Because they don't know anything about horses!" Cameron said, downing his orange juice. "I'd outgrown my pony and told them I needed a new horse. So they bought Paddy. The first time I got on him he bolted and kept going. He leapt over six fences and ended up two kilometres from my house before he finally gave up galloping. I thought, *well that proves he can jump*, so I started eventing him that season."

Cameron smiled at Georgie. "How's that wee Connemara of yours? He's a brilliant jumper!"

Georgie shook her head. "I'm on a school horse

now," was all she said. The last thing she wanted to do was discuss Tyro. That morning, she had called her dad and then Lucinda to let them know that she had arrived at Blainford. She had been desperate for news about Tyro, and was relieved when Lucinda told her that Tyro was settling in brilliantly at the Prescotts' farm in Northampton. She wanted Tyro to be happy, she really did. But mostly she wanted him to be here with her. When Lucinda asked about her new horse, she didn't say anything. Her trainer would think Georgie was bonkers if she told her that Belladonna might actually be her mother's old horse. She needed to talk to Tara first and find out the truth.

Alice looked up at the clock on the wall. "Ohmygod! Eight twenty-six! Come on, we better go."

"Hey! I still haven't eaten my toast!" Cameron complained, but no one was listening. They were already stacking their trays and heading for the door. It was time for school.

Chapter Ten

In Blainford's Great Hall the seats were already filling up fast. Georgie, Alice and Cameron grabbed a bench together at the back. On the stage, the staff of the school sat in rows of chairs on a raised platform. They were a rather odd bunch, some dressed in typical teacher's clothes, others dressed in jodhpurs or, in a couple of cases, cowboy chaps. At the front of the stage, behind the wooden lectern, stood a tall woman with stiff, erect posture and what could only be described as a long horsey face. She cleared her throat into the microphone and the room of 250 students fell silent.

"Good morning. For those of you who are new to the school and do not know me already, I am Mrs Dickins-Thomson, headmistress of Blainford Academy.

Welcome to our first assembly of the school year," she said.

"I would like to say a particular welcome to all our new junior pupils, who come here from every corner of the globe. Never forget that you are privileged to be accepted into a school where many of the world's greatest riders have learnt their craft."

The headmistress gestured to the wooden plaques behind her, each one shaped like a scroll with names written on them in large gold leaf lettering.

"Blainford Academy is more than just a school. This college has turned out more champions in its illustrious history than any other equestrian college. As you stand here today, take a look around you at the names that adorn the honour roll."

Georgie felt the hairs stand up on the back of her neck as she looked at the honour roll for 1987 and saw the name Virginia Lang in gold script. Lang had been her mother's name before she married and became Ginny Parker.

"Here at Blainford," Mrs Dickins-Thomson continued, "we expect every one of you to strive and excel in the great tradition of this academy so that one day, your own name will be included among our honoured graduates.

"Now," the headmistress smiled, "this week, the traditional Burghley – Luhmuhlen polo tournament will be held on Saturday on the school's number one polo field. Parents and supporters are welcome and as always we expect all pupils to attend. For those of you applying for the Calgary Rodeo this term, please hand your applications in to Mr Shepard, head of the Western department, by the end of class today."

Mrs Dickins-Thomson consulted the stack of papers on her lectern. "That brings us to the end of today's assembly. Morning classes will be running fifteen minutes late because of assembly and all students must go straight from the Great Hall to their first class. First year students – you will need to consult the yellow timetables you've been given with your stationery orders to find out where you need to go next. Now, will you all please file out in an orderly fashion."

In the stampede that followed, Georgie, Alice and

Cameron were nearly trampled by students elbowing and shoving their way out of the doors that led into the quad.

"Oh no!" Alice's face suddenly dropped as she emerged out of the doorway. She quickly turned around and tried to barge back past Georgie against the flow of human traffic.

"Alice?" Georgie squeaked. "What are you doing? We can't get back inside again."

"Kennedy alert!" Alice said desperately. "She's right in front of us!"

But it was no good. The unstoppable wave of students forced them into the quad and, despite her attempts to escape, Alice found herself coming face to face with Kennedy Kirkwood.

"Alice Dupree!" Kennedy said. "I was wondering if I'd see you here."

"Yeah, well, you've seen me now, Kennedy, so keep moving," Alice said darkly.

"Well, it's lovely to see you too," Kennedy purred, "I really didn't think you'd make the final cut. The last time I saw you I was kicking your ass at the auditions."

"You didn't kick anything, Kennedy," Alice replied through gritted teeth. "You only beat me by two points."

"Winners don't bother to keep count of the score," Kennedy trilled. Then she looked at Georgie and Cameron.

"Aren't you going to introduce me to your friends?"

"Georgie Parker and Cameron Fraser," Alice mumbled reluctantly, "this is Kennedy Kirkwood."

"Georgie Parker!" Kennedy tossed her glossy hair back. "I've heard of you. You aced the British auditions, right? You're Ginny Parker's daughter?"

"That's me," Georgie said nervously.

"It'll be good to have some real competition at last," Kennedy said. "It was a total non-contest when I won the US auditions. You know, they call this place the All-Stars Academy, but these days they let just about anybody enrol." She looked pointedly at Alice.

"What's your major?" Kennedy asked Georgie.

"Well, I'm taking eventing and dressage as my option classes this term," Georgie said, "but really I want to be an eventer."

"Oh, well, I guess you'll see me in class!" Kennedy

said. "I'm doing eventing too – my whole family are showjumpers, they think I'm crazy."

"Me too!" Cameron said.

Kennedy was taken aback.

"I mean, 'me too I'm an eventer'," Cameron added hastily, "I didn't mean I think you're crazy. I hardly know you. You might be crazy, but that's OK. I'm a little bit crazy too, so that's something else we have in common!"

"Who are you again?" Kennedy glared at him.

"Cameron Fraser," he grinned. "I'll be in your eventing class."

"Wow. Neat," Kennedy said sarcastically. She turned back to Georgie. "Well, like I said, it's good to have some real competition! See you at the stables!"

"Not if I see you first, super-witch!" Alice muttered under her breath as they watched Kennedy walk off. Then she turned to Cameron. "What was all of that stuff about?"

"I don't know," Cameron groaned. "Kennedy probably thinks I'm a babbling fool."

"Well," Alice mocked, "that's something else we have in common!"

✳

The new juniors had been split into three classes for morning subjects. Georgie, Alice and Cameron were all in 3A, which meant they had German for first period.

"Lateness will not be tolerated," Ms Schmidt said as they took their seats.

The German teacher didn't look much older than her pupils. She was tiny with big doe eyes and fine blonde hair. Although small in stature, she was a formidable horsewoman. She had once been the captain of the German Olympic team and her name was one of those in gold script on the honour roll in the Great Hall.

Ms Schmidt clearly didn't believe in wasting time. She began speaking to the class in German and Georgie, who had never taken a German lesson before, had no idea what was going on!

To make matters worse, the two girls in front of her, a German girl with a thick blonde braid by the name of Isabel Weiss, and a Dutch girl with braces and poker-straight brown hair called Mitty Janssen were both fluent German speakers. When Ms Schmidt asked

157

a question, Mitty and Isabel would reply in German! And Mitty and Isabel would be the first to raise their hands every time, sitting up ramrod straight in their eagerness to answer.

Georgie was beginning to see the school cliques emerging around her. Kennedy Kirkwood, who was also in their class, was whispering and passing notes with Arden and Tori. Despite the school rules about not wearing nail polish or jewellery, all three wore the same bright lilac polish on their nails and gold locket necklaces around their necks.

At the back of the room, slouching in their seats, chewing gum and pretty much ignoring Ms Schmidt, were four kids who looked like the Western posse. One of the boys, obviously the leader of the group, had shoulder-length blond hair and a fringe so long that you could barely see his eyes. He was lanky and lean and wore the sleeves of his school shirt rolled up to the elbow, exposing his tanned forearms.

"The Westerns?" Georgie whispered to Alice, pointing to the boy and his friends.

"Uh-huh. That's Tyler McGuane," Alice whispered

back. "We met at the US finals. He rides a palomino Quarterhorse. He's into barrel racing and that kind of stuff." She pulled a face. "He's OK, I suppose. You see that boy next to him with the dark hair in a braid? That's Jenner Philips, and the two girls are Bunny Redpath and Blair Danner..." Alice stopped talking immediately. She had noticed that the sharp eyes of Bettina Schmidt were trained upon her.

"Miss Dupree? Miss Parker? If you're talking then you've obviously finished writing down all your vocab words. If you want, I can always give you ten more," she said in a clipped voice.

"No, Ms Schmidt, I haven't finished," Georgie admitted.

"Then back to work!"

When Georgie had dreamed about coming to Blainford, she had never given any thought to what the actual schoolwork would be like. She realised now that she'd been expecting the lessons would be easy and the riding would be the tough part. However, in their next class the maths teacher, Miss Somerford, made it quite clear that academic brilliance was expected as well.

"You may think it is enough to be a good rider, but I can tell you that if you fail in my class you will have no future at Blainford Academy," Miss Somerford said as she wrote equations briskly on the whiteboard.

"Class rankings are given at mid-term and again at the end of term. You'll be given your grade and that will determine your ranking within the class in every subject."

Georgie could barely keep up just writing everything down. She had no idea what any of the answers were to the questions.

"Don't worry," Alice told her as they left class, "I happen to be a secret maths geek. I'll help you later when we get back to the boarding house."

Their third class that day was English with Mr Otto. The room was on the other side of the quad and Georgie walked there with Cameron and Alice.

Georgie watched Tyler McGuane walking just ahead of them. He had this really cool languid stride as if he'd just got off his horse and was about to walk into a saloon bar like they did in the movies.

In English class, Tyler made a point of sitting right next to Kennedy and Arden. He kept staring over at Kennedy and at one point he leaned over during class and asked to borrow her text book. She passed it to him without even acknowledging his existence.

"Tyler McGuane might be hot, but Kennedy Kirkwood would never give him a second glance," Alice announced. They were having lunch in the dining hall and Alice was taking great delight in explaining to Cameron and Georgie just how the cliques always worked at Blainford.

"Tyler's a Western rider," Alice went on. "Showjumperettes wouldn't be seen dead with a Western boy. They are totally into polo poseurs…"

"Speaking of polo poseurs," Georgie hissed, "Conrad Miller is coming this way."

As always, the other boys from Burghley House were with Conrad. They sat down at one of the empty prefect tables with their lunch trays but Conrad kept walking, heading straight for Georgie.

"Parker," he said coolly.

Georgie looked up. Conrad was standing over her.

"Don't forget, you've got fatigues today," he said. "Report to the stables at four o'clock after school."

Alice was convinced that Conrad had a crush on Georgie.

"Yay for me!" Georgie said sarcastically. "What are fatigues anyway?"

"Chores around the school," Alice said. "Whatever the prefects can find for you to do – like moving showjumps or cleaning out troughs."

"Again," Georgie groaned, "I'd just like to say, 'yay for me'."

The girls were walking back up the driveway towards the stables, having got changed into their jodhpurs and short boots. They were on their way to their very first ridden class of the new term. Eventing with Tara Kelly.

Georgie was feeling sick at the prospect of riding Belladonna. Alice wasn't helping calm her nerves either. As they caught up with Cameron on the driveway, Alice began telling horror stories about Tara Kelly's cross-country class. "Cherry and Kendal got eliminated from cross-country after the first term,"

Alice told them. "They both think I'm mad to take Voldemort's class after what they went through."

"Voldemort?" Georgie asked.

"That's what Kendal and Cherry called her when they were in her class because she's such a—" Alice slid open the sliding doors to the stables and saw none other than Tara Kelly herself standing right there!

But if Tara had been listening she didn't give anything away. She checked her wrist watch and looked up at them. "Time is tight, Mr Fraser and Miss Dupree!" she said briskly. "You'd better hurry up and saddle your horses." And then she turned to Georgie.

"And you, Miss Parker, need to come with me. I want to talk to you about your new horse."

After her first meeting with Belladonna yesterday Georgie had tried to convince herself that jetlag had been clouding her judgement and blurring her vision. But in the clear light of a new day, when the stall door swung open once more, nothing had changed. The mare bore the most striking similarity to Boudicca. Could they be one and the same?

"She's beautiful, isn't she?" Tara said, clipping the

lead shank on Belladonna's halter and leading her out of the stall. "I suppose you recognise her?"

"I… I don't know." Georgie was uncertain what to say. "I think I do."

Tara nodded. "I must admit I had my reservations about giving her to you. But I have this feeling that you two will click. She's a talented mare. Only six years old so she's inexperienced and green, but with the best bloodlines I've ever seen. She's the spitting image of her mother. So that makes two of you."

And at that moment the penny dropped. "She's Boudicca's foal?"

"That's right." Tara led the big bay around and tied her up to the hitching post. "Boudicca was bred at stud and had one foal before she was sold to your mother. This is that foal. I had the chance to buy her at auction six months ago, and I snapped her up, knowing that if she had half the talent her mother possessed she'd be perfect as an eventing mount for the school. She's been broken in and lightly ridden, but just like you, this is her first year at Blainford."

It all made sense to Georgie now. No wonder this

mare looked exactly like Boudicca! And her name Belladonna made sense too, as Warmbloods always kept their parents' initials.

"She's a complicated ride," Tara continued, "and normally I would give a horse like this to a more senior student. But I thought, considering your shared history, that you might like to try her. Of course, if you don't want to I can exchange her with one of the senior mounts…"

"No!" Georgie could feel a lump in her throat as she reached out and stroked the mare's thick glossy black mane. "No," she said again, more softly this time, "don't give her to anyone else. I'll ride her."

"Excellent!" Tara Kelly said briskly, handing Belladonna's lead rope to Georgie. "You'll find her tack in the shed. Be quick because you're due in class now."

In the tack room, Georgie found not one but two saddles on the racks in Belladonna's locker. There was a black SLK high-head Albion with a deep seat and long flaps for dressage. The second saddle was a honey-coloured Pessoa, smaller and more lightweight, a flat-seat saddle to be used for showjumping and cross-country Georgie picked up this one and carried it back.

As Georgie threw the numnah and saddle across Belladonna's back, the mare shuffled about anxiously. Georgie was just as nervous as her horse. Belladonna had yet to prove she had no vices. Georgie kept a close eye on the mare as she tightened the girth and then did up the nosebands and throatlash on the bridle, checked her stirrup length and followed Cameron and Alice who were already getting on their horses over at the mounting block.

"Are you coming? Class is starting soon!" Alice called as Georgie hesitated at the mounting block.

Georgie looked at the mare standing in front of her, then finally she put her foot in the stirrup and swung herself up into the saddle. Belladonna was a whole two hands taller than Tyro and it was a long way to the ground. Being on this mare made her feel like a child playing dress-up in her mum's high heels. After all, her mother had never let her on Boudicca. Now here she was, on a horse just as big and powerful and possibly even more unpredictable.

"Come on!" Georgie was shaken out of her thoughts by Alice imploring her to hurry up. "Tara's already got the other riders lined up. We're late!"

The three of them walked together across the field towards the arena. They arrived at the entrance gate just in time to see Tara bawling out Isabel Weiss. Isabel had turned up for class without her back protector or bell boots on her horse.

"Go to the stables and get them!" Tara commanded. Then she turned her back on Isabel and addressed the rest of the riders. "This goes for all of you! Do not expect to be allowed to ride if you're not in proper gear. Do I make myself clear? This isn't a ballroom dancing class. This is cross-country, the most dangerous sport in the equestrian world, and you must be prepared!"

As she said this, she caught sight of the whip in Mitty Janssen's hand. "Is that a dressage whip?" Tara was wide-eyed in disbelief. "Go back to the stables and swap to a proper cross-country crop! And be quick!" Tara yelled after them as they rode off. "We'll be waiting for you so we can start!"

She looked at Alice, Cameron and Georgie at the

edge of the arena, too scared to come in. "Ah, Miss Parker, Miss Dupree and Mr Fraser!" Tara slapped her riding crop against the palm of her hand. "Nice of you to join us at last! What are you three waiting for? An invitation from the Queen? Get in here and line up!"

Cross-country class was about to begin and Tara was already living up to her old nickname.

Chapter Eleven

*T*he eventing students stood nervously as their instructor paced in front of them with her riding crop clasped in her hands. "Welcome to cross-country class, novice level one," Tara Kelly said. "You have all gone through the most rigorous auditions to be accepted into this school. You have proven yourselves the best young talents from around the world…" She paused and took a long hard look at the young riders lined up in front of her. "…All of which counts for nothing in my class. You've been told you're the best? Think again. This is where the hard work really begins. You're about to find out if you're a true eventing rider. We will stretch your talents beyond the limits of anything you have experienced before and take your riding to a whole new

169

level. Some of you will find the pressure too much. This class has the highest drop-out rate in the school. Fifty per cent of my students will not make it to the end of the year."

The young riders looked terrified.

"As you already know," Tara continued, "class rankings happen at mid-term and then once again before the end of term. There are twelve of you in this cross-country class. All scores are accumulated towards your final end-of-year mark." Tara frowned. "If your rank falls to the bottom of the class then you will need to consider your future – or I will do it for you. I do not encourage students to stay in my class if I do not think they can perform. Cross-country is a dangerous business and I cannot afford to have riders out there attacking fences when they are off their game." Tara's eyes scanned the row of riders.

"If any of you here are half-hearted about this class then I suggest you leave now," she said.

Nobody moved. Tara had known that they wouldn't. She gave this lecture every year to her first year students. From this row of twelve young hopefuls she would try to create future stars of the international eventing world and the students in this new intake were some of the most talented that she had ever seen.

At the far right, on her hand-me-down horse, William the Conqueror, was thirteen-year-old Alice Dupree. Tara had taught both her older sisters, but they had failed to cut it as eventing riders. However, the youngest Dupree seemed to be made of sterner stuff than her siblings and there was something steely about her that Tara liked.

Next to Alice were two riders that Tara had chosen at the British auditions. Daisy King had a neat professional style but there was something about her dark determination that Tara found unnerving. Beside Daisy sat Cameron Fraser, a wildcard that Tara had convinced the other selectors to back. He lacked training and finesse but she liked his daredevil attitude and his natural bond with the big coloured cob he rode.

Tara had chosen dressage rider Isabel Weiss at the auditions in Germany. She was puzzled to see her taking part in the cross-country class, but impressed by Isabel's determination to push herself beyond her limits. She was uncertain about Isabel's choice of horse too, a heavy-boned brown Oldenburg. Although solid enough jumpers, Oldenburgs could be slow across-country.

Tara suspected that Mitty Janssen had only joined the class because she was Isabel's best friend. Mitty rode a dark brown Dutch Warmblood that Tara definitely liked much better as a cross-country prospect.

Emily Tait was next in line. The New Zealander rode one of the school horses, a jet-black Thoroughbred called Barclay. The boy next to her, Alex Chang, was Chinese, but spoke with an English accent. His mother was a diplomat and Alex had learnt to ride in Oxfordshire. His mount, Tatou, was an Anglo-Arab grey, which was unusual since the breed were commonly chestnut or bay.

To the right of Alex on a very glossy Selle Francais gelding was Nicholas Laurent. Nicholas had been in the French junior equestrian team before Tara had chosen him at the European auditions. There was already an arrogance to Nicholas, Tara thought, but rightly so. He was undoubtedly one of the best riders of the group. Beside him was another self-assured young rider, Australian, Matt Garrett, who rode a school horse, a handsome sixteen-two hand dun called Tigerland.

Isabel and Mitty weren't the only additions to the group that had surprised Tara. Kennedy Kirkwood had been a stand-out rider in the US auditions. She had star quality, no doubt about that. But she was a Kirkwood – a family with a showjumping heritage. Tara had not expected to see her in this class. Neither had she expected to see Kennedy's best friend and fellow socialite Arden Mortimer. It was a relief to see that Tori Forsythe had decided to stick with Miss Clairmont's turn-out classes instead of joining them.

Kennedy rode a powerful chestnut Selle Francais gelding called Versace while Arden rode a dark-brown Holsteiner mare called Prada. Tara couldn't help smiling at how perfectly the two horses suited these girls. Typical showjumperettes, she thought, choosing horses to match their hair colour.

The other English rider in the cross-country class was Georgie Parker. Tara had some misgivings about assigning Belladonna to the girl. The mare, like her rider, was green, but talented. If it worked then they would be unstoppable, but there was the risk that Belladonna could be too much horse for Georgie to handle.

"Right!" Tara said briskly. "Check your girths and take your stirrups up to jumping length. We'll warm up and take a look at your positions in the arena and then I'm going to take you out on the novice course. It features the smallest fences we have here at Blainford and should be within your capabilities. Your lesson in week four will be the first rankings test. You will be expected to get a clear round."

Tara saw the worried expressions on their faces. "I'm not making you ride the whole course today. We're going to tackle the difficult jumps on this course one by one." She paused. "Today we're going to be jumping the water complex."

The novice course was the smallest of the three cross-country courses, and its water jump was not much more than a large pond. It was less than half a metre deep all the way across – not enough, Georgie noted with relief, to get trapped underneath her horse this time.

The pond could be entered and exited in any number of combinations from all directions. If you trotted in from the north side you could ride straight into the water without jumping. Then in five strides, at a trot, you were through the pond and jumping up a metre-high wooden retaining wall on to the raised bank on the other side. Or you could take the same route in reverse, leaping off the bank into the water and then cantering out the other side. The easiest routes were to come at the water from the west or east side, jumping in off the low raised banks on either edge of the pond.

"I'm not going to give you any advice on how to approach this jump, or which route or angle you should take," Tara told the twelve riders. "I want to see the decisions that you make and gauge the kind of riders you are."

It turned out that the twelve riders were all very different indeed. Some, like Cameron Fraser, only knew one speed on a cross-country course – a mad gallop. Cam rode Paddy through the water and flew the large bank to get out again at top speed.

"You were lucky," Tara told him. "There was no control. If your horse had got into trouble you were powerless to adjust his stride. Try it at a trot next time!"

"I don't think Paddy knows how to trot!" Cam muttered to Alice and Georgie as he rejoined the other riders.

Kennedy Kirkwood had ridden the water next and Tara had been complimentary as Kennedy took the easy route from west to east. "Nicely done, good canter stride and strong body position."

Of all the riders who followed, only Nicholas Laurent and Daisy King took the water the hard way, jumping down off the big bank and cantering through and out the other side.

As Georgie rode forward to take her turn, she was determined to take this chance to prove herself. Even though she was on an untested novice mare, she decided she would go one better than Nicholas and Daisy, by taking the riskiest of all routes into the water, the big leap into the pond off the high bank, topped by a sudden turn to canter out again, jumping over one of the low banks. It was an option that demanded precise control and courage and no one had attempted it so far.

"Go ahead when you're ready, Georgie," Tara called out.

Georgie was surprised when the mare set off like a bullet. There was no way she could hold Belladonna back as she fought for her head and came in at the water complex at a mad gallop, far too fast to take the big drop into the water. Georgie was still trying to slow her down when Belladonna approached the jump. She stood up in her stirrups and then, just as Georgie was preparing for the mare to leap, Belladonna didn't. Instead, she shied violently to the left and Georgie flew over her head and into the pond. As she emerged from the water muddy and soaking, the only thing Georgie felt was embarrassment.

"A bit ambitious perhaps," was Tara's assessment as Georgie climbed up the bank looking like a drowned rat.

"Miss Kelly?" Kennedy piped up gleefully from the sidelines. "Perhaps she should wear a snorkel instead of a hard hat next time?"

"That's not funny," Tara said firmly as Kennedy and Arden sat there giggling.

"Try that again please," Tara told Georgie. "But bring her in the easy way this time, we don't want her to get phobic about water jumps, OK?"

Sodden and humiliated, Georgie clambered back into the saddle. As she approached the low bank, Belladonna still raced it but Georgie was ready for her this time. She hung back and sat heavy with a gruff growl and managed to ride Belladonna successfully into the water and up the other side.

"That's it everyone!" Tara said. "Back to the stables."

There is nothing worse than the clammy feeling of riding in wet jodhpurs. As she rode back humiliated and shaking, all Georgie wanted to do was get her horse unsaddled and go back to the dorms.

"That was quite the performance." It was Kennedy Kirkwood. She slid down off Versace and stood next to Georgie. "Is that how you won the UK auditions? Did you do a little synchronised swimming or did the judges let you in for performing backstroke?" she said snidely.

"Shut up, Kennedy!" snapped Alice. She had a

furious look on her face as she defended her friend. "It's her first day on a new horse and she's got jetlag."

Kennedy shrugged. "I thought you'd be my rival, Parker. I guess I was wrong about you."

"Why don't you join Miss Clairmont's lessons now and stop wasting everyone's time," Arden joined in. "If you learn to do nice plaits I might hire you. I could do with a new groom."

As the showjumperettes walked away giggling, Alice and Cameron closed ranks around Georgie.

"I'll take care of Belladonna for you," Cam offered, "if you want to go and get changed."

"Thanks," Georgie said, "but you heard what Arden said. Untacking and grooming horses may be my new career once I fail this class."

"Who ever listens to anything Arden says?" Alice said dismissively. "She's Kennedy's lapdog. She only barks when she's given permission. And as for Kennedy, she's like a hyena. She looks for the weakest one in the herd and tries to drag them down. But if you ignore her she'll pull her claws in and move on to someone else."

Georgie felt terrible. Back home in Little Brampton she hadn't exactly won any popularity contests, but no one had ever bullied her. And when it came to riding, she had always been the most fearless one on the cross-country course. It had, without a doubt, been one of the worst days of her life. "At least today's over," she said to Alice as they slid their saddles back on to the racks.

Alice screwed up her face. "Ummm… have you forgotten?"

"Forgotten what?" Georgie asked.

"Georgie, it's four o'clock. You've got to go to the Great Hall and meet Conrad. You're on fatigues."

Chapter Twelve

After her disastrous cross-country lesson, Georgie had dutifully reported for fatigues and found herself in a field for the next two hours with a pitchfork in her hands, picking up horse dung and wheelbarrowing it to the compost heap as Conrad told her to "put some effort into it".

As she dragged herself back to the boarding house that night, aching, smelly and utterly miserable, Georgie decided that this was rock bottom. Life at Blainford could not get any worse. But then that was before she had natural horsemanship classes with Miss Loden.

Natural horsemanship was one of the compulsory subjects at Blainford. "Call me River," the teacher told them at the start of their lesson. River Loden didn't wear jodhpurs and a hard hat. She wore sage-green cotton harem pants and rope sandals and her wrists were strung with silver horse charms. She smelt of pennyroyal flowers and her long curly dark hair was tied back with a lavender twist.

"Today," River told them, "we'll be exploring our relationship with our horse by sharing our ch'i."

Ch'i, River explained to the class, was life energy. "The essence of our bodies, expressed by our breathing, just like transcendental yoga," she said, twirling her hands as she spoke. The class spent the next hour breathing up their horses' nostrils trying to share their ch'i.

"It's an ancient natural horsemanship practice," River insisted. "If you breathe gently up the horses' noses, it will calm them."

Alice wasn't so sure. "I think Will could do with a breath mint!" she hissed to Georgie.

Georgie decided to give the breathing her best shot, but after half an hour of inhaling and exhaling and getting nothing but baffled snorts in return, she was ready to mount up.

River Loden, however, had other ideas. "Groundwork is very overlooked," she told the riders. "There's no need to ride the horses. We're going to spend the rest of the afternoon on the ground doing rope work to improve our personal space and help our relationships."

They spent the rest of the lesson with the horses in halters and lead ropes, teaching the horses to take a step back if they gave the rope a vigorous wiggle. Georgie couldn't believe it. "I fail to see how this is going to help me get a clear round on the cross-country course," she muttered.

River Loden, who had ears like a bat, overheard and floated over to her like a sage-green cloud. "I should have known I had some eventing students in this class," she said softly. "You're the ones with the prickly energy. It's always the same. You're the hardest to convert to natural methods. You have very rigid ideas about what being a horseman means. You need to expand your minds."

Kennedy Kirkwood was not convinced. "I'll expand my mind when she shrinks those pants," she muttered to Arden. "Harems are so over."

At the other extreme, dressage class the next day with Bettina Schmidt was like being put through army bootcamp. From the moment the riders were mounted up and in the arena Bettina was barking orders at them. She wore a headset with an amplifier strapped to the small of her back so that the riders could hear without her shouting – but she managed to shout anyway and her instructions never stopped. She made them ride non-stop for two whole hours, spending half of that time with the stirrups crossed over at the front of the saddle so that the riders had to cope without them.

"You will never master sitting trot if you do not let go of your dependence on stirrups and relax your thighs!" Bettina asserted as the riders bounced around the arena.

Georgie wanted to point out to Bettina that it was hard to relax your thighs when you were on a brand new horse that was prone to bolting off at full gallop. Belladonna had the most enormous trot stride that was almost impossible to sit to. But it was clear that no one talked back to Bettina and so she clung on and survived the two-hour ordeal.

"I think that sitting trot has loosened my fillings," she groaned to Alice as they dismounted and took the horses back.

Alice was walking with her legs apart like a cowboy. "The first hour was painful enough," she said, "but the second hour gave pain a whole new meaning."

Thursday's class was Western Compulsory with Hank Shepard who had a leathery tan and wore a Stetson atop a lustrous wave of grey hair. His handlebar moustache flicked up at the corners, making it look like he was always smiling. He sat on the fence post by the arena and twirled his lasso at his feet in slow languid loops as he talked.

"Y'all can call me Shep," he told the students.

"This guy is going to be another rope wiggler like Loden," Alice whispered to Georgie. But Shep didn't believe in rope wiggling or groundwork.

"For your half-term exam you'll need to know how to rope a steer from a gallop," he told them. "So let's get started. I've got two dozen cattle in the chute ready to go."

Isabel Weiss was horrified. "My Oldenburg has never even seen a cattle!" she told Georgie with wide eyes. "He is a purpose-bred dressage horse with outstanding bloodlines, worth a fortune, and this cowboy expects me to chase these beasts with a bit of rope?"

Tyler McGuane and Jenner Philips were the first volunteers to try out. Both of them made it look easy, galloping down hard after the steers when the chute opened, roping their calf around the horns and flinging themselves off their horse to plant the beast on the ground and hogtie its feet. Despite being half the size of the boys, Bunny Redpath and Blair Danner also managed to rope and pin a steer each. Their horses were brilliant at cattle cutting and the girls did fearless leaps from their backs to wrestle the calves to the ground, hogtying them briskly and stepping back with hands raised so that Shep could clock their time.

Arden Mortimer was the first non-Western to give it a go. When the chute opened her Holsteiner took one look at the calf and reared back. Arden shrieked and dropped her lasso on the spot.

"I broke a nail on that stupid rope!" she scowled, as she held up her lilac fingertips. After that, she refused to try again.

None of the other non-Westerns fared much better. Cam, who fancied himself as a bit of a cowboy, rode hard after the calf and even managed to get the rope around its neck, but instead of tying the end to his pommel horn he had mistakenly tied it to his own belt. As the steer took up the slack he was yanked out of his saddle and got dragged along the ground for the length of the round pen before Shep could cut him loose.

Georgie felt sick with nerves when she was in the chute waiting for her turn. When the gates opened she managed to keep Belladonna alongside the steer long enough to throw the rope but missed the horns entirely.

At least she was trying. Kennedy seemed entirely preoccupied with Westernising her Blainford uniform by knotting the shirt at the waist to show off her tanned midriff and Nicholas Laurent made a half-hearted attempt, tossing the rope in the air as if he didn't care.

"We have cattle on my farm at home," he told Shep sniffily, "but in France we do not chase our cows with silly ropes."

Matt Garrett, the Australian rider, seemed to cope the best. His lasso was wonky but he managed to get it over the steer's head and wrestle him to the ground. "We've got a cattle farm too, in Coober Peedy," he told Nicholas.

"How big is your farm?" Nicholas asked. "We have over two thousand acres in the Dordogne."

"Mate! We have two hundred thousand acres," Matt replied. Nicholas looked impressed until he added, "Mind you, most of it is desert. There's more snakes than cows on our place."

Friday afternoon's showjumping class seemed to be the only thing the showjumperettes had talked about all week. Georgie realised something strange was up when Arden refused to put her helmet on before class. When one of the other riders mentioned that being on her horse bare-headed was against the rules she snapped at them. "I don't want to squash my blow-dry before Trent gets here!"

Alice rolled her eyes. "Arden, put a helmet on before your brain falls out." She turned to Georgie. "The showjumperettes are all in love with Trent."

It was easy to see why. In his taupe polo breeches, white shirt and tobacco-coloured Dubarry boots, Trent Chase looked like a movie star – all tanned skin, wavy brown hair and perfect white teeth. He was the youngest teacher at Blainford and he'd already competed in the USA World Equestrian Games.

"He's also a ten-goal polo player," Alice told Georgie. "Honestly, if those showjumperettes could use a lasso properly I swear one of them would throw a rope around Trent Chase!"

Despite his too-handsome-for-his-own-good charm, Georgie liked Trent Chase immediately. The instructor had a direct, no-nonsense approach to showjumping that reminded her of Lucinda. They spent the day doing gridwork. Trent had set up a long alley of small fences down the middle of the arena. The grid began with trotting poles and progressed to cavaletti, finishing off with three higher jumps constructed with coloured rails. The horses all followed each other through the grid in single file with Trent calling out to the riders to work on their rhythm and maintain a steady unchanging position.

After their mad galloping display at the water complex, Georgie had been nervous that she would have problems jumping Belladonna. But working with other horses in front of her meant that Belladonna couldn't just gallop off. Forced to slow down she actually relaxed and took the showjumping grid in her stride, performing brilliantly.

"Fantastic riding, Georgie!" said Trent, singling her out. "You can tell that you're Ginny Parker's daughter – you ride just like your mother. She was always a hero of mine."

Kennedy was far from impressed by the attention that Georgie was getting. "Just because Trent has some sort of Ashton Kutcher complex about your mother, doesn't mean you can out-jump me," she said in front of the others as they were hacking back towards the stables. "I won my place at this school as a showjumper and when the mid-term exam comes I expect to be in the number one spot."

It wasn't like Georgie even particularly cared about showjumping. The only class that mattered to her was cross-country, and right now she was at number twelve. If she didn't improve her performance then she would be kicked out.

✳

On Saturday morning, Georgie sat at the edge of her bed having a total crisis. "It's no use," she told Alice. "I give up!"

"Georgie, you're making a fuss over nothing."

"I'm not!" Georgie insisted. She had been so preoccupied with her riding classes that she hadn't noticed that the rest of the girls at the school were all concerned with something much more important – the upcoming polo match. Or, more specifically, what they were going to wear to the polo. Now at the last minute, Georgie was having a wardrobe meltdown.

"I have nothing to wear. I thought we'd be in our uniforms. I didn't know we'd be expected to wear our own clothes to the polo match. I don't have anything that looks right!"

Alice held up a floral sundress still on its hanger, smoothing it against her body as she looked at herself in the full-length mirror. "It's no big deal," she said distractedly, "you can just borrow something of mine."

"Really?" Georgie couldn't believe it. Alice had the best wardrobe. She had that sort of effortless bohemian style that off-duty celebrities have in magazines.

"Here," Alice picked a dress off the bed, "this should fit you."

It was a pale yellow cotton sundress with shoestring straps. Georgie pulled it on and looked in the mirror. The yellow dress suited her fair freckled skin and her blonde hair and its frills looked cute on her lanky, boyish figure.

"Really? Are you sure it's OK for me to wear it?" Georgie said gratefully.

It felt strange to be walking up the school driveway in pretty dresses. Daisy, who was wearing a plain blue dress and plimsolls, spent most of the walk complaining bitterly that she didn't see why they couldn't wear jodhpurs. Isabel, Emily and Mitty were all excited about seeing a polo match for the first time.

It was a hot, sunny day and marquees had been erected along the sidelines of the polo field to provide shade for the spectators. Already the first marquee was filling up with students, teachers and parents as well as old boys from Burghley and Luhmuhlen who had come to watch this traditional grudge match between the two boarding houses.

"Is Cam coming?" Georgie asked as they grabbed a table in the second tent. "Should we save him a seat?"

"Cameron is riding!" Alice told her. "He's in the Luhmuhlen team."

"I didn't know Cam played polo!"

"He doesn't really," Alice said, "he only joined the team this week." She tried to explain. "Polo teams need to contain a mix of four riders with different handicaps, and since Luhmuhlen has two superstar players with ten-goal handicaps, they needed Cameron to even out the team handicap. He's a minus-two goal player, so it all balances out. If you know what I mean."

Georgie didn't have a clue what she was talking about, but it sounded complicated.

"You'll understand once they start to play," Alice

said as they sat down.

As the four Luhmuhlen players took to the field, Cameron rode out amongst them on a chestnut pony with a hogged mane, bandages on its legs and a strapped-up tail. It was funny how different he looked in his polo uniform. The tight white polo breeches, knee pads and long leather boots made all the boys look smart as they cantered along. Cameron managed to look slightly less smart when, showing off his skills to the girls in the stand, he took a warm-up swing with his mallet and gave the ball a massive whack. It flew straight at the main grandstand and into the crowd, narrowly missing Mrs Dickins-Thomson and Mrs Dubois who were engrossed in conversation as the ball whistled between their heads.

"Sorry!" Cameron winced. "Just getting the hang of it. My first game."

Looking far more suave and clearly knowing exactly how to swing a mallet was their eventing classmate, Alex Chang. "Alex has a three-goal handicap," Alice told the others. "That's pretty good for his age. He played for Oxfordshire in their last big game."

194

When the Burghley team came out, Georgie instantly recognised Nicholas Laurent. He was by far the youngest player on their team. Conrad Miller was team captain and he came out first, waving his polo mallet menacingly as he galloped his grey pony down to the far end of the field. Beside him was Andrew Hurley, also a prefect with sandy hair and dark eyes. He yanked his horse about brutally as if he was steering a motorbike rather than a live animal. As he galloped by, Georgie remembered that he had been one of the boys who had stood back and sniggered when Conrad had given Georgie fatigues for walking on the quad.

When the fourth member of the Burghley squad rode on to the field Georgie felt a rush of excitement as she recognised James, the blond boy with the high cheekbones and lopsided grin. If she had thought he was handsome before, now dressed in polo kit, his eyes the same colour as Burghley's ice-blue shirt, he looked devastating.

"Do you know who that rider is on the Burghley team?" Georgie asked.

"Which one?" Alice peered at the pitch. The riders were all cantering their horses back and forth, getting ready for play to begin.

"The one next to Conrad—" Georgie began and then suddenly the whistle pierced the air. The game was underway! Like bolts of lightning the riders began tearing down the pitch at breakneck speed.

"Go Cam!" Alice shouted. "Go Luhmuhlen!"

"Are we supporting Luhmuhlen House then?" Daisy asked. She was intensely grumpy at the notion of watching other people ride. "I don't see why it's just the boys' houses. Why aren't girls playing?"

"Because it's a traditional grudge match!" Alice answered. "And of course we're cheering for Luhmuhlen. There's no way I'm cheering for Conrad."

Georgie had never watched a polo match before. She had always imagined it might be a bit like hockey on horseback, but it wasn't. It was more like rugby combined with horse racing and was the most thrilling and exhilarating sport she had ever seen. The riders barged each other with their horses, fighting to get to the ball and then, once they had broken free of the pack,

196

they rode at full gallop swinging their mallets to take a shot at goal.

Cameron seemed to have found his ideal sport. His fearlessness and tendency to ride his pony hell for leather made him a natural on the polo field. He made up for taking a pot shot at the headmistress when he scored the first goal of the game. He gave Georgie and the other girls a wave as he celebrated by cantering across the pitch with his mallet held aloft.

There was another goal soon after that from Burghley and then another one from each team before the whistle went. The game had only been going for seven minutes and already the players were leaving the field!

"Is that it?" Georgie asked. "It seems kind of short."

"That was a chukka. They play six chukkas in a polo match," Alice explained. "After each chukka the riders leave the field and swap on to fresh horses."

"How do you know so much about polo?" Georgie asked Alice.

"My dad loves to play. He owns a couple of strings of polo ponies," Alice said as if this were no big deal, even though a 'string' meant six ponies!

"Your dad owns twelve polo ponies?" Georgie tried not to look too astonished. She knew that her room mate was wealthy but she had no idea how rich. It wouldn't be until she got back to the dorm and took off the yellow sundress that she would see the double C logo on the label and realise it was from Chanel.

A few minutes later the players were back on the field again. The day was getting really hot. Georgie understood now why each player needed six ponies. A seven-minute chukka, with its mad gallops and sharp turns, must have been the equivalent of running the Grand National.

Another goal was scored by both teams and as the third chukka got underway the scores were tied at three-all. On the sidelines the team coaches were anxiously watching.

"That's Heath Brompton," Alice pointed out the house master from Burghley who also happened to be Blainford's polo instructor. On the other side of the field Trent Chase, the Luhmuhlen coach, stalked the sideline, watching as his team let another goal through to make the score four-three to Burghley.

The third chukka was in the final minute of play when Conrad made an attempt on goal and Cameron nearly got his head lopped off by Conrad's mallet as he tried to stop him.

"Foul!" Alice was shouting out. "The ref should have picked that up! Conrad is such a cheater!"

A few seconds later, Conrad had another shot at goal and this time his aim was true. At the end of the third chukka, half-time, Burghley House were in the lead, five goals to three.

Georgie watched the riders canter off the field. Her eyes were fixed on James as he took off his polo helmet and wiped the sweat from his brow. Her heart sank when he vaulted down off his horse and was greeted by Kennedy Kirkwood!

Kennedy smiled at him and took the reins of his pony. She was wearing a knock-out red dress that was so tight it clung to every inch of her.

"Check out Kennedy Kirkwood's outfit!" Emily said. "Did she think she was coming to a polo match or performing in a Lady Gaga video?"

Georgie sighed, "The polo boys don't seem to mind it."

"What boys? You mean James?" Alice looked at Georgie as if she was a bit dim. "Is he the one you meant to point out before?"

Georgie nodded. "Yeah... so he's Kennedy's boyfriend?"

Alice shook her head. "That's James *Kirkwood*," she grinned. "He's Kennedy's brother."

Chapter Thirteen

Georgie felt irrationally thrilled that James and Kennedy weren't boyfriend and girlfriend. "James Kirkwood is cute," Alice agreed. "Trust me, you're not the first one to notice it. The showjumperettes in his year are totally obsessed with him."

While the polo players prepared for the next chukka, the girls headed out on to the field to stomp divots. "You push the sods of grass that have been dug up by the ponies' hooves back down again to smooth out the pitch," Alice explained. "To help the ball roll smoothly across the grass in the second half."

"So we don't get to actually ride, but we have to fix the playing field?" Daisy was incredulous. "This is a total waste of time. I could be training right now instead of wearing this dumb dress and walking around pushing dirt with my feet!"

The other girls began leaping about in fits of giggles, racing each other to see who could push the divots back into place the fastest.

"OK," Daisy said. "If we're going to do this then let's have a proper race to see who can stomp the most. First one to a hundred wins. Ready? Get set, go!"

"six... seven... eight... nine..." Georgie was so focused on the grass beneath her feet she wasn't paying attention and the next thing she knew she had barged straight into someone.

"Ohmygod! I'm really sorry..." Her heart skipped a beat as she looked up into James Kirkwood's blue eyes.

"Parker!" He gave her a lopsided grin. "Having trouble with the grass again?"

"What...?" Georgie was bewildered.

"Conrad gave you fatigues for walking on it. Now you mow me down trying to stomp on it."

"I'm so sorry..." Georgie began.

"Don't worry," James added. "I don't mind if you run me over. Although if you jumped on top of Conrad like that I can assure you it would be a different story…"

James tucked his polo helmet under one arm and raked his damp blond hair back casually with his hand.

"So how many goals are you, Parker?" he asked her.

"Huh?"

"You know, as a polo player," James said.

"Oh!" Georgie blushed. "I'm no goals. I've never played polo."

James looked surprised. "I thought since you came from England and all that you would play."

"Not in Little Brampton!" Georgie laughed. "We don't have a polo team. Not even water polo."

"You know they have a girls' team at Blainford if you want to join," James told her. "I could teach you the basics some time if you like. I've been playing since I was little. My dad was Burghley's team captain when he rode here."

"So do you major in polo?" Georgie asked.

James shook his head dismissively. "Nah, I play a little but I'm really a showjumper. What do you?"

"James!" They were interrupted by a shout across

the polo field, and Georgie turned to see Kennedy, Tori and Arden walking together towards them.

"Hey, Kennedy," James smiled, "you know Parker here, don't you? I was just telling her that I'd give her a polo lesson some time if she wanted."

Kennedy rolled her eyes. "Oh, James, don't be lame. That is so cheesy, offering to teach her how to play polo!"

Kennedy flicked her hair back and smirked at Georgie. "She's not your sort of girl anyway. Did you know she rides a school horse?"

"Wow, Kennedy," James shook his head, "all those years of charm school that Mom and Dad paid for have really been wasted on you, haven't they?"

Kennedy shrugged nonchalantly. "Whatever, James. You can date whoever you want, but I'm just warning you. She can't ride – she's flunking Tara Kelly's class. And she doesn't even have her own horse. She totally doesn't deserve to be at Blainford."

"Did you actually want something, Kennedy, or did you just come over here to tell me who I can't be friends with?" James asked her archly.

"I came to tell you that Mom and Dad have arrived," Kennedy said. "They're over at the champagne marquee with the Mortimers. They want to see you – don't ask me why."

James sighed. "I better go," he told Georgie and he walked off towards the far side of the field, leaving Kennedy, Tori and Arden behind.

The showjumperettes stood there, staring haughtily at Georgie and the others who were finishing their stomping game.

"You're not stomping divots," Alice pointed out to them.

Tori pulled a face. "These shoes are Roberto Cavalli. You don't stomp in Roberto Cavalli."

Isabel and Mitty came over to join the others. Kennedy took one look at Isabel's dress, a white cotton shift with embroidered flowers around the neckline, and laughed.

"Hey, Heidi," she giggled. "Lost your goat herd?"

Tori and Arden sniggered and poor Isabel looked really upset. She had told Georgie and the other girls that morning that this was her favourite dress and that her mum had made it especially for her to take away to school.

Georgie thought fast. "I can't believe you don't realise, Kennedy," she said airily. "That's a Mikkel Van Meester dress. Totally cool. There was one on the cover of *Vogue* last month. Didn't you see it?"

Kennedy frowned. "I don't remember that."

"Ohhh!" Arden said. "I've heard of Mikkel Van Meester!" She cast an admiring gaze at Isabel's white smock. "It's amazing! You're so lucky."

Kennedy still looked suspicious. Georgie could tell that she'd be getting her stack of *Vogue* magazines out when she was back at Alberta House that evening, but right now the head of the showjumperettes didn't want to look uncool.

"Yeah, it's cute," Kennedy had to concede. She turned to Arden and Tori. "Come on, let's go get something to drink."

As the showjumperettes wobbled off across the grass in their high heels, Isabel looked at Georgie with total gratitude. "Thanks for making up that stuff about my dress and sticking up for me," she said.

"It was nothing," Georgie said.

"No," Isabel replied. "It was something. It really was."

✳

On Monday in the dining hall Georgie was just sitting down with Alice, Mitty and Isabel, when Kennedy walked over with her tray and slapped it down on the table with a face like thunder.

"Do you want to sit with us?" Mitty asked innocently.

Kennedy gave a hollow laugh. "Do I look like I want to catch loser flu?" she said. Then she narrowed her eyes at Georgie. "Very funny. Your little joke on Saturday? I've looked through all my back issues of *Vogue*. There is no Mikkel Van Meester."

The whole table looked up and they all began to giggle. Kennedy's expression grew even darker. "I don't know what you're laughing at," she snapped. "Especially you, Parker. Cross-country class is this afternoon and you are the biggest loser. When the mid-term exam comes I'll be the one laughing and you'll be gone. Game over."

✳

Tara Kelly was in a brisk mood as she met the riders out on the novice cross-country course. "We only have two classes left before the exam," she told the eventers, "and we have lots of ground to cover. Today, we're going to focus on one of the most technical elements on the cross-country course." She paused. "We're going to be jumping the coffin."

"Geez," Alice groaned. "Did Dracula name these jumps or what? Whose creepy idea was it to call a fence the coffin?"

"It's because the ditch at the bottom is low in the ground and narrow like a coffin," Cam told her. "They're a really common cross-country jump."

"Have you ever jumped one?" Alice asked.

"No," Cam admitted. "But it can't be that bad."

Neither of them had noticed the look on Georgie's face. When Tara told them they'd be jumping the coffin she had turned as white as a sheet. That was the jump that Ginny Parker had fallen at on that fateful day at Blenheim.

Georgie knew that Boudicca had somehow lost her footing coming down the bank and flipped into the ditch with Ginny Parker underneath her. Now, Georgie was facing a similar obstacle, mounted up on a mare that had hardly any brakes and liked to gallop her fences.

"You must not gallop this fence." It was as if Tara Kelly was reading her mind.

"Coffins are a complex obstacle and require precision riding," Tara told the class. "It is vital that you stay in canter and give your horse time to look at the jump and negotiate the three elements. Clear the log, then your horse will put in two strides down the bank, pop over the ditch and do two more strides back up the bank, over the next log and out the other side. It's vital to get your timing right and maintain your speed. Get it wrong and break into a gallop and you'll be in big trouble."

"Georgie?" It was Cam. He could see how terrified Georgie was and he looked really worried about her. "Are you OK?"

Georgie took a deep breath. "I'm fine," she insisted.

"Mr Fraser!" Tara called out. "Since you're obviously so clever that you can chat to other riders instead of paying attention to the lesson, I think we'll have you through first please!"

Tara watched as Cameron circled Paddy around and prepared to tackle the jump.

"No galloping remember, Mr Fraser. A slow impulsive canter is required. Keep your horse collected underneath you, give him time to look at the jump.

"Too fast!" Tara told Cameron as he came towards the first element. Paddy clearly wanted to bowl at the jump in his normal fashion but Cameron managed to check the big cob just a couple of strides out from the fence then let him go again. Paddy flew the first log, took two neat strides, popped the ditch and then put in two more strides uphill and back out over the second log.

"Textbook stuff, Cameron," Tara said. "I hope everybody was watching that carefully because that is how I expect all of you to handle this obstacle. I cannot repeat enough that you mustn't rush this fence. It is tempting on a cross-country course to let our horse stay in a gallop over jumps to make better time and indeed some fences can be taken at a gallop. The coffin is not one of them!"

Kennedy Kirkwood was up next. She rode Versace in a perfect straight line and took the log in a forward stride, then down and over the coffin and up the other side, making the whole jump look effortless. She had a smug look on her face as she pulled up in front of the others – as if to say "beat that".

Alex and Nicholas followed after that and went through with no trouble. Alice had a moment's hesitation at the first log and Isabel and Mitty both had refusals the first time but Tara made them try again and they were soon confidently riding all three elements. Then came the three riders on school horses. Both Matt and Emily did surprisingly well, considering neither of them were really accustomed to their mounts. Matt was actually bragging about this to Nicholas until Tara overheard him and put him in his place.

"You've had a week now with Tigerland," she said coolly. "Mark Todd only had two hours on Horton Point before he rode him at the Badminton Horse Trials and won it. I think managing your way over a novice

211

cross-country fence hardly rivals his achievements."

Then it was Georgie's turn. "When you're ready, Miss Parker, can we have you through?" Tara called out.

Georgie thought she was going to throw up. She had never felt quite so ill about taking a jump in her life.

"Georgie," Tara seemed to sense her hesitation, "I want to see some positive riding here. Don't stand off too much because if she jumps long you'll end up with the wrong striding coming into the ditch."

As she turned Belladonna and cantered the mare back around towards the first log, Georgie tried to keep all of this in her head. She tried to ride 'positively', but fear was overriding her system, driving out any rational thought and replacing it with mind-numbing terror. Belladonna meanwhile could see the log ahead and she surged forward, breaking out of a canter into a gallop.

Georgie gave a hard tug back on the reins and sat up but it didn't make any difference. Belladonna was galloping and showing no signs of slowing down. Georgie completely lost it. Convinced they were going to crash, she could see only one solution. She needed to bail out.

Hauling with all her strength at the left rein she pulled Belladonna off course, intentionally dragging the mare from her line, swerving away from the jump. With the eyes of all the other riders on her, Georgie pulled the mare up to a halt and then turned and came back to face Tara Kelly.

"What went wrong?" Tara asked her.

"I had to pull her off," Georgie replied. "There was no way she could take it at a gallop."

Tara looked disappointed at this response. "You could have easily checked her back to canter before the jump. You had plenty of time. Try again, and this time keep her at a steady canter from well out and use lots of right rein to correct her in case she goes to the left again."

"No," Georgie said. Her face was white with terror and her eyes were teary. She gave them a hasty wipe and shook her head. "I'm not doing it."

"What?" Tara wasn't accustomed to students talking back. "Georgie, you can't let the mare get away with this or she'll learn bad habits. You have to take this jump again right now."

"No, I don't. And don't bother to tell me some story about what Mark Todd did at Badminton because my mum took this jump at Blenheim and she never came home. So don't lecture me about what I should do because I don't care!" Georgie shouted. "I'm out."

The whole class watched in disbelief as Georgie cantered off, heading back towards the stables.

Georgie was shaking as she rode Belladonna back. She had never lost her nerve like that before. It was hard to explain but she knew in her heart that there was no way she could have taken the jump. As she rode across the fields, she took one last look around the stately grounds of the academy. It was a farewell of sorts. She wasn't going to be riding here ever again, because Georgie Parker had made her mind up. She wasn't just leaving Tara's class. She was leaving Blainford.

✳

Back at the dorm room, Georgie dragged both her suitcases out from beneath the bed and began to empty

214

her clothes out of the wardrobe. She had already filled one case and started on the next when Alice arrived.

"This is crazy," Alice said. "You're leaving school?"

"There's no reason to stay." Georgie threw a T-shirt into her suitcase. "I'm at the bottom of the class. If I don't go then Tara will just kick me out anyway after the exams."

"So what if you fail eventing? Just swap to another class!" Alice said. "There's no need to go all drama queen and quit school!"

"OK, so if I stay and fail eventing then what subject do you suggest I fill my new timetable with?" Georgie shot back. "Grooming and plaiting? I came to Blainford to be an eventing rider and if I can't do that then there's no reason to be here."

Alice had no comeback. She knew she would feel the same way. "I wish you weren't doing this," she said as she helped Georgie to pick up a T-shirt that had gone flying in her mad packing frenzy. "I thought we were going to be, like, best friends."

"I know," Georgie said softly, "me too. I guess some things just don't work out the way you want."

Georgie couldn't face dinner that evening. How could she tell her friends that she was going to be the first one to fail Tara's class?

"Can you tell Cam and everyone else goodbye for me once I'm gone?" Georgie had asked.

Alice reluctantly agreed that she would. Tomorrow, Georgie would call Dr Parker so he could arrange the details with Mrs Dubois. Her dad would no doubt be thrilled that she wanted to come home and Georgie would be on the next flight back to England.

There was just one more goodbye that she needed to do before she left. And so that evening, while everyone else made their way up the driveway to dinner, Georgie waited and then set off towards the stables.

As she walked down the corridor towards Belladonna's stall, she was thinking how different things could have been if only she had brought Tyro with her. He would have been a superstar in the cross-country class. But Belladonna was headstrong and difficult, and Georgie simply never clicked with her the way she had with the black Connemara.

Belladonna heard Georgie's footsteps in the corridor and stuck her head over the Dutch door to nicker a greeting. The mare was so like Boudicca, with those deep expressive eyes and that white heart marking on her forehead. *Beautiful to look at,* she thought, *but just like Boudicca – impossible and dangerous to ride.*

"Georgina?" She heard footsteps and a voice behind her in the corridor and turned round to see Tara Kelly standing there.

"Why aren't you at dinner?" Tara asked.

"Not hungry," Georgie shrugged.

Tara looked at her. "I was hoping we'd have a chance to talk after you stormed out of my class today."

"I didn't... I didn't mean to be disrespectful. I just couldn't do it any more," Georgie said. She took a deep breath. "I'm going to quit the class. I'm going to leave the academy and go home. I don't think I'm cut out to be an eventing rider after all."

Tara's face fell. "Are you serious? This is a very big decision you're making. Have you really thought this through?"

Georgie nodded. "Blainford's not what I expected it to be. I always wanted to come here and be a really great eventing rider like Mum..." she trailed off. It was too painful to say the rest. Kennedy had it right – Georgie wasn't good enough to be here. She was out of her depth.

Tara unbolted the stable door and gestured for Georgie to come back out.

"We need to talk," she said.

"It's about your mother."

Chapter Fourteen

*T*ara took Georgie to the tack room and sat her down while she made them both a cup of tea. It wasn't until Georgie took the mug from Tara's hands that she realised how much she was shaking.

Tara sat down in the seat opposite Georgie. "You know that your mother and I were very competitive with each other when we were at school?"

"Uh-huh." Georgie hesitated. "Lucinda said that you and Mum didn't really get on."

Tara arched a brow. "That's fair enough I suppose. I guess that's how most people saw it. Tara and Ginny, always at each other's throats. Each of us determined to be the best.

"Ginny and I were rivals," Tara said, "but we were

friends as well. We brought out the best in each other. When I was competing Ginny was always the one rider I would strive to beat, someone to measure my achievements against." She took a sip of tea. "Competition here is tough but it makes you a better rider. You'll find the same thing once you settle in at Blainford."

"No, I won't." Georgie was fighting not to cry as she spoke. "I'm not like you and Mum. I don't have what it takes."

Tara shook her head in disbelief. "Georgie, you've only given it two cross-country lessons! Your mother arrived here like you, expecting to be an instant champion on her first day on the cross-country course and instead she was in the bottom half of the class for the first two terms. I seem to recall her spending half her time on her backside in the middle of the water complex."

Georgie couldn't believe it. "You're kidding me!"

"Have you ever known me to joke about anything?" Tara said flatly.

"But the way Lucinda talks it's like Mum was this golden girl right from the start."

"Lucinda was your mother's best friend," Tara said, "and memories play strange tricks on us. We only remember the good times. Yes, by the time she was in her senior year at Blainford, Ginny Parker was a superstar. But not at first. She had to fight her way to the top, and stay strong and focused when things got tough."

Tara looked at Georgie. "That's what she would want you to do right now. Stay here and fight. She wouldn't want you to give up just because you've had a few setbacks. You're too good for that, Georgie." Georgie was shocked by Tara's praise. The steely instructor had never said anything so complimentary to her before.

"I'm not making you any promises about your future though," Tara said. "You've got mid-term exams in two weeks' time and if you don't do well then you're up for elimination just like everyone else. I don't play favourites in my classes, Georgie. If you fail the exam you'll be gone."

Georgie bit her lip. "What about Belladonna? If I stay would I keep riding her?"

"That's up to you," Tara said. "I know that the mare has been difficult so far. I never said she was an easy ride." She paused. "I gave you Belladonna because she's the most promising horse in the stables. She's not a push-button ride by any means, but I'm confident you can handle her. But it's your decision. If you want to change horses, I can arrange that."

"No," Georgie shook her head emphatically. "No, it's OK. I don't want to change horses. I want to ride Belladonna." She took a deep breath. "And I want to come back to cross-country class."

"Excellent!" Tara stood up. "Well, I'll see you in the arena next week then?"

She put her cup on the bench and was about to leave when Georgie called after her.

"Tara?"

"Yes, Georgie?"

"Thank you."

Tara smiled. "Don't mention it." And then she added, "Seriously, don't mention it. To anyone. I don't want my image to be tarnished. I've worked hard to become She Who Must Not Be Named. I don't want you ruining my reputation." And with that she walked out of the tack room, leaving Georgie sitting there in gobsmacked disbelief, gripping a cup of cold, untouched tea.

✳

"You've changed your mind? You're staying?" Alice couldn't believe it when she came back from the dining hall to find Georgie's clothes unpacked, the suitcases back in storage under the bed again.

"What happened?" Alice asked.

"It's a long story," Georgie told her. "Let's just say that an old friend of my mother's convinced me to stay."

Alice let loose a loud shriek and rushed across the room to give Georgie the most enormous hug.

"This is it, OK?" she said. "You are never allowed to scare me like that again. You're my best friend and you have to stay here and stick it out with me, no matter what."

"Urghh," Georgie said. "Alice, I promise not to go anywhere, but can you stop hugging me now?

You're squeezing the life out of me!"

"Oops!" Alice disengaged from her embrace. "Sorry! Don't know my own strength."

Alice was still over-excited the next day. When they joined Cam and Alex for breakfast she had a huge grin on her face.

"What's up, Alice?" Cam looked at her. "You're acting weird."

"I was just thinking it's so great to have Georgie here!" Alice said.

Cam stared at Alice as if she was bonkers. "Yeah, it's totally amazing. Can you pass the sugar, Georgie?"

"Sorry," Alice told Georgie as they left the dining hall on their way to class. "I know I sounded nuts in there – I'm just so glad you changed your mind."

✳

Later, sitting Miss Somerford's Tuesday maths class, already confronted with a fiendishly difficult mock exam as prep before the mid-terms, Georgie wondered if she had made the right decision after all. Having been given the first week to settle into their routine the students were now expected to be up to speed with their studies and the workload was intense. And at Blainford the pressure to be the best was enormous.

Georgie was doing two hours of study each evening just to keep from falling behind. She had been one of the brightest in her year at Little Brampton. But things were different here in Lexington. They were very different indeed.

✳

"We're going to begin the lesson as always by channelling our energies with some deep breathing exercises!" Miss Loden told the class brightly.

Instead of sage-green harem pants, River Loden wore saffron cotton muslin wrapped around her in a complicated origami. She had bare feet and no helmet, which once again horrified Georgie who had spent her entire life being told not to enter stables without her hard hat and a pair of sturdy boots.

At least once the breathing exercises were out of the way today Miss Loden had promised they would actually be riding. Georgie remained sceptical about this since it was their second lesson and they hadn't got on their horses so far. But after half an hour of swapping ch'i with their horses, Miss Loden finally said it was time for the arena.

"Fear is our subject for the day," she addressed the class as they stood there with their horses tacked up ready to ride. "I'd like you to put your hand up please if you have ever been afraid of a horse," River said.

The pupils all looked uncomfortable. No one dared raise their hand.

"I'm feeling negative energy here," River said, opening her palms out to the class. "Be honest. Share your deepest feelings."

A few of the riders reluctantly raised their hands.

"Fear is natural," River reassured them, smiling beatifically. "It's instinctual. Every day we ask you to climb on top of an animal that is three times your size and ten times as strong, and we expect you to show no fear. But fear is there, in all of us." She stepped forward towards the riders and smiled at Georgie. "I'm getting interesting vibrations from you, Georgie. I think you and Belladonna should be my subjects for this demonstration."

River Loden took the mare's reins and led her forward then beckoned for Georgie to follow her. They were standing out in front of the class so that everyone could see them. Georgie could see Kennedy and Arden at the back of the class giggling.

"Horses can sense fear in their rider," River continued. "People talk about that as if it's some magical sixth sense that they possess. But in fact there's no great mystery to it. When we're scared our bodies act differently. Instead of sitting up straight, fear makes us instinctively hunch over and grip with our thighs. For a horse, who can sense the most minuscule shift in balance on its back, these are physical cues that something is very wrong. If you're afraid then your horse naturally assumes that they should be worried too."

Emily Tait raised her hand timidly to ask a question. "So it's the rider's fault if their horse is afraid?"

"Yes... and no," River replied. "These situations are a vicious circle. You pass your fear on to the horse, then your horse acts badly, refusing to jump or bucking and rearing and then you become even more afraid. You may even fear your horse when you are on the ground, in the stall or in the paddock. The fear can begin anywhere."

Listening to River's explanation it suddenly became clear to Georgie. From the moment she first encountered Belladonna there had been an element of fear between them. Georgie's courage had left her that first day at the water complex and things had got worse ever since. Belladonna reminded her so much of Boudicca, and after what happened to her mother Georgie was scared the same thing was going to happen to her too.

It was Georgie who had panicked at the coffin, not Belladonna. The mare had simply been reacting to Georgie's own fears.

"So how do you stop it?" Georgie asked. "How do we get rid of the fear?"

"Free your mind and your body will follow," River said enigmatically. "Can you mount up on to Belladonna please?"

Georgie put her foot in the stirrup and sprang up on to the mare. River passed her a black scarf. "Put on this blindfold."

Georgie's eyes widened. "Why? What's going on?"

"Don't look so frightened!" River smiled. "I know you're an eventing rider and you're opposed to my horse-whispering tricks. I promise you there's nothing mystical about this."

Georgie tied the scarf around her eyes while River slipped a lunging cavesson over Belladonna's bridle. "Don't worry," she told Georgie, "I will be holding on to the lunge rein the whole time that you're blindfolded so I will have total control of your horse.

"Is the blindfold on tight enough?" River asked. "You're sure you can't see?"

Georgie nodded. She was totally blind. River made a clucking noise with her tongue and Belladonna moved away and began to walk on the circle around the trainer.

As Belladonna walked around on the lunge rein, River explained what she was doing to the rest of the class. "This is an effective way of making a rider aware of what fear does to their body and correcting their position again as quickly as possible," she said. "Without our eyes to guide us we gain true vision."

River looked at Georgie who was still circling on Belladonna's back at the end of the lunge rein. "Feeling OK?" River asked.

"Yes," Georgie said nervously.

"Excellent. Let go of the reins," River told her. "I've got the lunge rope so nothing can happen to you. Now place your hands down so they are resting on your thighs."

Georgie did as she said and River continued her instructions. "Focus on your body position. Are you sitting straight or are your shoulders hunched?"

"I'm hunched," Georgie said. She straightened up her back, surprised at the new-found physical awareness she had now that she couldn't see. She felt vulnerable up there on the horse but free as well. Without her vision her other senses were taking over. She was suddenly aware of every muscle and every bone in her body.

River kept a tight hold of the lunge rein. "OK, Georgie, stand up in the stirrups and when you sit down, rebalance those seat bones." Georgie did as she asked. "Now put your hands straight in front of your

230

face with your fingertips stretched out towards Belladonna's ears," River told her. Georgie did this. She was beginning to think this riding blindfolded business was easy. Until River said to prepare to trot.

"On the count of three. One… two…" Georgie almost panicked and ripped the blindfold off on the first few trot strides. But River kept giving instructions, telling her to put her weight in her heels and relax, and soon she found her balance. Before she knew it, Georgie was riding around the arena doing a rising trot with no reins, completely blind. Beneath her she could feel Belladonna's magnificent floating paces as the mare sped over the surface of the sand arena.

After they had done a few circles at a trot, River slowed them back down and brought Belladonna to a halt. "I'm just setting up a little jump," she told Georgie. "It's not very big, only half a metre off the ground. I'm going to set it up and get you to canter this time."

"What!" Georgie felt her heart racing. This was madness!

"Control your fear," River said in a lilting, soothing voice as if she were a hypnotist rather than a riding instructor. "You can do this."

As Georgie and Belladonna were sent back out on the lunging rein, Georgie focused all her energy on relaxing and doing exactly what River Loden told her to do. "Loosen your thighs, straighten your shoulders, sit up and get ready to canter," River instructed. Georgie did as she said and felt the most amazing sensation as Belladonna began to canter. She was in total darkness and the horse was flowing beneath her. She could feel their energies merging.

"You're about to take the jump now," River told her. "Get ready... and one, two, three!" Georgie felt the horse rise up underneath her and she instinctively moved with her. She felt the wind in her face and then the jolt as they landed again on the other side. Then River was calling the mare down to a walk and telling Georgie to remove the blindfold. They had done it!

"You can see," River told the class, "how Georgie is sitting better in the saddle now. Taking away our sight makes us feel so much more deeply. We all ride better if we let our fear go and concentrate on our riding instead." River Loden turned to the class. "Now, who's next?"

Over the course of the lesson the whole class had a turn at blindfolded riding. Georgie, meanwhile, focused on using her new-found position to school Belladonna. She worked her at a walk, trot and canter until she felt like she really had the measure of the mare and Belladonna was responding neatly to her aids.

"She's going much better for you," River Loden said approvingly. "She can sense your confidence. She's not spooking any more."

Under River's watchful eye, Georgie asked Belladonna to canter again. "Stop holding her back," River instructed. "Ride forward and let her go." Georgie did as she said and the mare began to really stretch out and show off her elaborate paces.

"See how beautifully she moves?" River smiled.

Georgie beamed as she urged the mare on into a powerful extended trot down the long side of the arena. Belladonna snorted and arched her neck, cantering a figure of eight like a dressage superstar.

"Not many horses can be so graceful in dressage, strong on the cross-country and then have the speed and agility required to be equally brilliant in the showjumping ring," River told Georgie. "This mare has talent in all three phases. Brought on correctly she could be the perfect eventer."

"How do you know this stuff?" Georgie asked. "I thought you were…"

"A rope wiggler?" River Loden smiled. "I'm a former three-day eventer. But I changed paths.

"I know you have your heart set on eventing, Georgie, but don't close your mind. You're here to learn everything there is to know about horses and the road to the top at Blainford is never straight. The trick is knowing which twists and turns to take."

Chapter Fifteen

Over the rest of the week Georgie grabbed every spare moment to train with Belladonna. She still found the mare a complicated ride. Belladonna was headstrong and hard to hold back but at the same time could also be sensitive to the slightest touch on the reins. After River Loden's lesson with the blindfold Georgie got into the habit of closing her eyes in the saddle, just for a moment whenever the mare was tense, and more often than not Belladonna would relax again and begin to respond to her rider.

It was working. Day by day, Belladonna was relinquishing her secrets to Georgie, and the girl was listening all the time, trying to figure out what made her tick.

Georgie would sometimes skip lunch in the cafeteria, taking a sandwich and a cereal bar from the boarding house and spend the hour with Belladonna grooming her instead. This was partly to avoid James Kirkwood, who she hadn't spoken to since Kennedy had put an end to their conversation at the polo, but mostly so she could spend as much time as possible with the bay mare.

One afternoon, when their riding class had finished, Georgie stayed behind with Alice to pull the horses' manes, combing and yanking out the hairs by the roots to shorten the mane and ready it for plaiting. You would have thought this would have hurt the horses, but Belladonna actually liked having her mane pulled and almost went to sleep while Georgie worked her way up the neck.

"I'm thinking of changing her name," Georgie admitted to Alice. "Belladonna is a bit of a mouthful."

"How about just shortening it to Bella?" Alice suggested.

"I don't know." Georgie pulled a face. "It's a bit *Twilight*, isn't it?"

Alice shrugged. "Then how about Belle? You know, like a Southern Belle? I don't think you should change it completely. It's bad luck to change a horse's name." She said this last part with such conviction that it was clear she had been through a bad experience in the past.

"OK then," Georgie said, "Belle it is."

"It means beautiful in French, doesn't it?" Alice said. "And she's a very beautiful mare."

"She is, isn't she?" Georgie agreed. As she said this, she felt her heart swelling with pride. Her beautiful mare. She was finally beginning to feel like she and Belle were developing that special bond with each other.

That weekend, there was polo on the main field on Saturday, a round robin tournament between various teams from Luhmuhlen, Lexington and Burghley. This was not a grand event so there were no marquees and champagne this time. "We're going to go and watch anyway, though," Alice told Georgie. "The trials for the girls' teams begin after half-term and I might pick up some playing tips."

Alice looked in the bedroom mirror and pushed a

straw Stetson down on top of her jet-black hair. "I'm meeting Emily and Daisy at the field, do you want to come with me?"

"OK," Georgie said. If Burghley House were playing in the polo then the chances were that James Kirkwood would be playing. Georgie hadn't spoken to him since the match that first weekend. Maybe James Kirkwood didn't want to have anything to do with a girl who couldn't afford to bring her own horse to the academy like Kennedy had said. She had seen James around the school since then, but he was always with the same gang of boys from Burghley. Not that she wanted to talk to him anyway. The last thing she wanted was for James Kirkwood to think she was turning up just to see him.

✳

"He's not here!" Georgie's eyes scanned the field as the eight players came out for the next chukka. James wasn't amongst them and she couldn't see him over at the rails with the polo ponies either.

"Who's not here?" Alice said. Then she clicked.

"Ohmygod! You're not still crushing on James Kirkwood."

"No!" Georgie said defensively. "I mean, maybe just a little…"

Alice raised an eyebrow at her.

"All right!" Georgie admitted. "I still think he's totally hot."

"He is totally hot," Alice agreed. "And he is also a Kirkwood. And in the year above us. And he's Kennedy's brother…"

"And," Emily added, "he's coming over this way!"

"Quick!" Georgie said. "Act like we haven't been talking about him!"

Alice looked bewildered. "How do we do that?"

"Hey, Georgie." James gave her that lopsided killer grin. He was obviously playing in the round robin because he was wearing his white polo breeches and house colours.

"Oh, hey, James," Georgie said, "I didn't notice you here. I was so busy watching the game."

"Oh, you're busy," James said. "That's a shame."

"No!" Georgie said. "I'm not really. Why?"

"I was just wondering," James said, "if you wanted to be my stick chick, you know, come and pass me my mallets and hold my horses while I play."

Georgie's face fell. "I get it," she said, "I'm too poor to bring my own horse to school cos I'm not a trust fund kid like you, so that means I'm only good enough to be your groom."

"What?" James's easy-going smile disappeared. "I didn't mean that. I just wondered if you wanted to…"

"Well, I don't," Georgie snapped. "I'm at this school to ride, not to brush and saddle up other people's horses."

James raised his hands up to calm her down. "Fine, I get it. Forget I asked, OK?"

He turned round and strode off back towards the polo ponies. Georgie watched him leave, still fuming at the nerve of him.

"What are you doing?" Alice rounded on her. "What's wrong with you? I thought you liked him."

"Yeah, but I don't want to be his 'stick chick',"

Georgie said, doing sarcastic air quotes with her fingers.

"Georgie!" Alice shook her head in disbelief. "Polo boys always get their girlfriends to be their stick chick. It's supposed to be romantic."

"You're kidding me."

"James Kirkwood just asked you out and you rejected him and called him a trust fund kid!"

Georgie groaned. She couldn't believe she'd blown it so badly. "Should I go over and apologise and tell him I'll groom for him?"

"Too late," Alice said. "Somebody has beaten you to it."

James was standing next to a grey horse, strapping on his knee pads, and there was a girl holding the pony for him. As James took the reins from her, Arden Mortimer looked ridiculously pleased with herself.

"You've driven him into the arms of Arden," Alice said melodramatically.

"Very funny, Alice," Georgie said darkly.

"He probably just chose her because he really

needed someone to be his stick chick for him," Emily offered kindly.

"Really?" Georgie said. "That's not what Alice said when he asked me though, is it?"

✳

So far Georgie's two encounters with James on the polo field had both been disasters. But at least they made for funny emails to send to Lily.

I don't know how I feel about him, Georgie wrote to Lily that evening. *He's totally part of a different clique to me and his snotty sister is so awful, but he is sooooo cute and seems really nice! It is totally confusing!*

I cannot believe how similar our love lives are, Lily wrote back. *Yesterday in biology class we were dissecting frogs and Craig Borell threw his frog's legs at me. At the time I thought "eww yuck frog!" but now I see that, really, I should have thrown them back as a sign of my mutual devotion. If only I'd done that – we could be engaged by now!*

Georgie took the point. Just because James had asked her to brush his pony was no sign that they were destined to be together. She needed to stop obsessing about him. Which wouldn't be difficult since she was certain he wouldn't want anything more to do with her.

Her other emails home to Lucinda and her father didn't mention the polo, or James obviously. She wrote to her dad about the looming mid-terms, assuring him that she was studying hard. Her email to Lucinda was less confident.

Tomorrow is the last cross-country class before the exams, she wrote. *We've been practising all the jumps on the course, but you know what Tara is like, she always manages to pull something at the last minute...*

Georgie was right. Tara Kelly was about to change the game.

✳

"As you all know," Tara addressed the eventing class, "the mid-term exam is next Monday. This year I'm setting an exam that will incorporate the jumps that we've been practising and will also test your boldness and speed across country."

Tara looked at the expectant faces in front of her. "We're riding a point-to-point," she told them.

Most of the riders looked back blankly. It was clear that none of them, with perhaps the exception of her British pupils, Georgie, Daisy and Cameron, had even heard the term before.

"A point-to-point is a steeplechase race over open countryside," Tara continued. "You won't be riding one at a time, taking your turn like a regular cross-country. You'll all race as a pack. There will be a three-kilometre race over open ground at the start, with hedges and low gates to hurdle, and then in the final quarter you will tackle three cross-country fences. They will be a real test, not only of your ability but also your endurance levels. By the time you reach them, you'll be tired and the fences will be a tough challenge for both horse and rider."

Tara didn't tell them which cross-country fences they would be jumping, but Georgie figured that the water jump and the coffin must be on the list.

"The first rider to cross the finish line will take out the number one place in the class ranking," Tara told them. "And the last rider will face elimination."

✳

"Do you think Tara is really going to get rid of one of us?" Emily asked as they sat in the dining hall after class that evening.

"She doesn't make jokes, remember?" Georgie pointed out. "The last one across the line will be first to leave the class."

No one felt much like eating. The other girls had already risen from the table and Georgie was following after them when Kennedy accidentally-on-purpose got in her way.

"Oh hey, Georgie," Kennedy said. "I was just saying to Arden and Tori that it's going to feel so strange in class after next week once you're gone. You know, when you come last in the point-to-point and get eliminated."

Georgie tried to ignore Kennedy and step around her, but when the showjumperettes formed a barricade and blocked her path Georgie finally lost it.

"You know, Kennedy, ever since I got here, all I've heard from you is how you came top of your auditions and how much better you are than me," Georgie said. "Isn't it about time you stopped talking about it and actually proved it?"

Georgie's voice was so loud it had silenced the dining hall. Everyone was staring at them. Kennedy's face dropped.

"Let's make a bet," Georgie said. "If I beat you in the class ranking, then you have to muck out Belle's stall for the rest of the term."

Standing beside Kennedy, Arden and Tori giggled nervously. The whole room waited for Kennedy to speak. James, who was seated at a table on the far side of the room, was watching and listening with an amused expression. Conrad Miller, meanwhile, looked totally astonished.

Kennedy regained her composure and gave Georgie a smug look. "You want to bet on it? Well bring it on, Little Miss Britain's Got No Talent," she said. "Why not? I just hope you shovel dung better than you ride. Parker, you're going down. And when you do the whole school is going to be watching."

Georgie slammed her dinner tray into the stack and turned on her heels. "I'm not planning on losing, Kennedy, so you better get your pitchfork ready."

As she stormed out of the dining room, Georgie

could sense that Conrad Miller was right behind her but she didn't care. She was standing up to the Blainford cliques and fighting back. Defiantly she swung the door of the dining hall open and kept walking straight ahead on to the grass.

"Parker!" She heard Conrad Miller shouting after her. "You're on the quad again. You've got fatigues."

Chapter Sixteen

Once the rest of the school heard about the showdown in the dining hall the eventing class exam the following Monday became a must-see event. Any students with a spare period that afternoon gathered on the novice cross-country course to watch the competition.

The course had been pegged out with red flags and the first two and a half kilometres of the steeplechase phase ran around the perimeter of the school along a broad flat track mown through the fields of long grass. Jumps were natural obstacles, hedges and stone walls that divided the fields, plus a few extra ones that had been specially erected. After the horses and riders had ridden this phase they looped back towards the cross-country course to jump the final three fences. As

Georgie had expected, these included the trakehner over the ditch, the water complex, and then finally the coffin.

It was a glorious sunny day and the spectators were finding shade and staking out vantage points at strategic trouble spots where the action looked set to happen. Most of them were gathering around the coffin, clearly convinced that this would be where the most thrills and spills might happen as the riders barrelled home for the finish line.

The coffin was still Georgie's bogey fence. She had yet to successfully get Belle over it. She remembered that Lucinda had once told her it was easier to jump bogey fences when you were out competing as your blood was up and adrenalin was pumping. She hoped her trainer was right. Her heart was hammering in her chest as she rode Belladonna out to join the rest of her classmates at the start line.

The twelve eventing riders were all seasoned cross-country competitors, but none of them had ridden an event quite like this one before.

"I feel like I'm entered in the Grand National!" Cam

said as he walked Paddy around, trying to keep the coloured cob calm.

The riders all wore their Blainford uniforms with numbered bibs on their chests so that Kenny, who was helping out today, could keep track of the order in which the riders crossed the finish line. Georgie gave Kenny a wave and Blainford's driver came over to say hello.

"Now this here is more like it!" Kenny said brightly. "This is a real horse race."

Kenny looked around to see if anyone was nearby and then he leaned over and whispered to Georgie, "Don't tell Miss Kelly, but I'm running a book on it. There's been some big bets laid."

"So who are they betting on?" Georgie wanted to know. "Who is the favourite?"

Kenny spat out his tobacco and looked around the field where the riders and their mounts were circling, preparing for the race.

"That chestnut over there," he pointed across the field, "he's got the most money riding on him."

Georgie looked over where Kenny was pointing. The chestnut was Versace.

✳

This was not the Grand National. There were no starting gates here today for the horses to enter, no metal cage. Instead, there was a rope. It was stretched across the start line and two senior boys from Luhmuhlen House held either end.

"Can the riders all line up, please," Tara called out.

Georgie had been planning to slot into line beside Alice and Cam, but Belle had other ideas. As the other riders urged their horses forward into line, the big bay mare tensed up and began to crab-step anxiously, moving sideways away from the rope.

"Come on, Belle," Georgie was firm with the mare, trying to kick her forward, but the whites were showing in Belle's eyes. She was starting to panic.

"Kenny!" Tara called out. "Can you lead her up?"

Kenny jogged over and clasped a leathery hand around the mare's reins. "Easy there, girl," he said gently to Belle. Reassured by the handler's confidence and the gentle sound of his voice, Belle stopped resisting and let Kenny coax her forward.

251

The other riders were all lined up at the rope now and the only gap remaining was between Daisy and Nicholas. Kenny eased Belle in between Daisy's big grey and Nicholas's Selle Francais. He looked up at Georgie. "They'll break pretty quick when that gun goes," Kenny told her. "You might want to grab yourself a hunk of mane and hang on so you don't get left behind." He let go of Belle's reins and gave Georgie a nod. "Good luck."

Now that the horses were all in place Tara Kelly raised the starter's gun and counted them down. "On your marks and three... two... one...!" The shot rang out, the rope fell and the twelve horses all lunged forward in unison. As Belle broke from behind the rope, Georgie was glad she'd taken Kenny's last minute advice. She had buried her hands in the mare's mane and stayed with the big bay as she hit her stride. Now, as the mare galloped forward, Georgie rose up on her knees in two-point position and tried to wrestle Belle back under control. She didn't want to let her gallop too hard, too soon. They were in a good position, not at the front of the pack, but about halfway back as the first jump loomed ahead of them.

It was a spar that ran between fields, a low rustic rail. There wasn't enough room for twelve horses to jump it at once and it became clear to Georgie as they bore down on the fence that some horses and riders would get pushed back in the crush.

As they came in to take the spar, Georgie sat back a little to let Belle know that the fence was coming. The mare sensed the change in her rider and gathered herself ready for the jump. They were only a couple of strides out when Georgie felt a heavy weight ramming against her leg, pushing Belle sideways beneath her and driving them out to the left.

Beside her, Daisy King was coming through fast on Village Voice and she had shoulder-charged into Belle to get the mare out of the way.

"Hey!" Georgie yelled as she was pushed off course.

Daisy didn't even turn her head to see what the aftermath of her actions might be. She had her game face on and her eyes remained utterly focused on the jump ahead.

Georgie managed to straighten Belle up and still take

the jump, but she had lost her striding and was now much further back in the pack. Daisy, meanwhile, was barging to get ahead once more, this time pushing Nicholas out of the way. Georgie heard Nicholas mutter something in French and then take a swipe at Daisy with his riding crop.

Georgie watched Village Voice's grey rump rising and falling as she galloped a few lengths in front of her. Daisy was riding to win and she was dangerous. Georgie needed to get past her and out of harm's way if she didn't want to get shoved around again.

Leaning low over Belle's withers she let the reins loose a little. Belle jumped on a forward stride over the next fence and as they landed Georgie urged the mare on, manoeuvring to the right so that she was riding in between Daisy and Nicholas. In four massive strides Belle had pulled up on Village Voice so that they were racing neck and neck. Then, before Daisy had the chance to ram into them again, Georgie asked for even more speed from Belle and the mare surged forward. In a few strides they were out of Daisy's reach.

They had got to the halfway point in the race now.

About a dozen lengths in front of her Georgie could see Matt leading the field on Tigerland. Breathing down his neck was Cam who was urging Paddy on for all he was worth. Emily was there too on Barclay. She was sitting steady and calm on the big black horse, riding like a professional jumps jockey, barely moving as they leapt the hedges and letting the horse maintain a steady stride. At the back of the four horses was Kennedy on Versace. The chestnut looked full of running as he flew the fences.

Belle was gaining on the leaders, her huge stride swallowed the ground and it didn't take long to close up the space so that they were on Kennedy's heels. Georgie could feel Belle flattening out and galloping even harder and as they approached the next jump they were almost neck and neck with Kennedy. Belle and Versace were matching each other, stride for stride. Georgie could feel the bay mare straining beneath her. Belle was looking Versace in the eye almost as if she was taunting the big chestnut. As they reached the next jump, a hedge, she was edging slowly but surely ahead. They would pass Kennedy and Versace in the next straight.

The body blow came out of nowhere. One minute Georgie was standing up balancing in the stirrups with the wind in her face and then suddenly she felt a thrust delivered sharply to her shoulder, and was knocked sideways out of the saddle. The next thing she knew she was falling. The grass on the other side of the hedge rushed up to meet her and she barely had time to prepare for the impact. She hit the dirt hard and the wind was knocked out of her. She gasped like a goldfish, trying desperately to get air back into her lungs.

"Georgie! Get down!" She heard Alice's cries as her friend rode over the jump and breezed right past her, and then she realised that there were more horses to come after Alice. The thunder of hooves was growing louder, coming nearer. The other riders who had been behind her in the field were bearing down on the jump. Unless she got out of the way they would be jumping right over the top of her!

Georgie looked up. They were just a couple of strides away. There was no time. All she could do was fling herself closer to the hedge and huddle beneath it, curling into a foetal position and staying as low as she could. As the hooves flew overhead she shut her eyes and tucked her head to her knees. She could sense the horses above her and for a brief second she peeked up and saw the belly of an enormous brown horse soaring directly over her.

And then the thunder was gone and Georgie was left alone, curled up and shaking. She was in shock but had no doubt about what had just happened. As they had taken the hedge, Kennedy had reached out and deliberately pushed her off her horse in mid-air. It was a crazy thing to do. Georgie could easily have been killed – if not by the fall itself, then by the galloping horses that had ridden directly over her head just a few seconds afterwards.

She didn't have time to dwell on what had happened. There was someone there now, standing over her on horseback. "Come on!" The voice was urgent and demanding. "Get up and give me your hand."

It was Isabel Weiss. She was mounted up on Leo, her enormous brown Oldenburg gelding, and was stretching her arm down towards the girl on the ground.

"Give me your hand!" Isabel commanded again. And this time, Georgie obeyed. Blonde and petite, Isabel was stronger than she looked. She yanked Georgie up off the ground as if she were a rag doll. "Stick your foot in my stirrup, quickly," she instructed, "and get on behind me. I'll double you."

Georgie was confused. "You can't double me all the way round the steeplechase!"

"I know that!" Isabel said. "I'm taking you to your horse! She's over there!"

Belle was standing by the next jump, grazing. She must have spooked when Georgie had fallen but she wasn't hurt.

"Come on," Isabel was getting hysterical, "we need to catch them up then you can finish the race." Isabel hauled Georgie up so that she was sitting behind her on the Oldenburg's broad back. "Now put your arms around my waist and hang on!" Isabel growled.

"I don't get it," Georgie said as they cantered together across the field towards Belle, "why did you stop to help me? There's no way you can win it now!"

"I am a dressage rider," Isabel said. "Eventing, cross-country, these things do not mean so much to me. But I know how much they mean to you. I know that you cannot afford to be eliminated."

They had reached Belle's side now and Isabel pulled her horse up so that Georgie could dismount. "Besides," she smiled at Georgie, "I want to see Kennedy Kirkwood's face when you cross the finish line ahead of her."

Up in the distance, Georgie could see the stragglers at the back of the pack. If she rode fast enough then hopefully she could catch them, but the fall had cost her valuable time.

"Thanks," she said to Isabel as she mounted up.

"It was nothing," Isabel smiled.

"No," Georgie grinned back, "it was really something."

Back in the saddle, Georgie knew she couldn't afford to slow down at the jumps. She urged Belle on into a gallop to take the next jump and then leant low over the mare's neck and threw the reins at her.

"You want to gallop, don't you?" she whispered to Belle. "Well, I'm not holding you back any more. This is your chance. Come on, go!"

Belle could see the pack up ahead of her and she was gaining on them quickly, her strides devouring the ground beneath her.

Directly ahead of them now was Arden, who'd had a refusal at the wire fence and was trailing the pack. Not far ahead of her was Matt, who had been in the lead most of the way, and had pushed Tigerland too hard and too soon. The big dun horse was now exhausted and falling back beside Arden. Georgie and Belle passed both of them at the next fence. Belle was fit and full of running.

By the time she came through the last steeplechase jump she had Alex and Alice in her sights. They were her friends but she had no choice. They were standing between her and Kennedy.

Alice gave her a wave as she sped past her, and she knew there were no hard feelings. Alex seemed shocked when he saw Georgie pull up alongside him, but he wasn't one for dirty tricks. And besides, Georgie hadn't actually beaten him yet. There were still the three jumps to come.

The first proper fence, the trakehner, now loomed a hundred metres ahead and Belle was still pulling. Georgie's hands were rubbed raw through her gloves from holding on to the mare in the early stages of the race and she knew she didn't have the strength to fight against her any longer. She let Belle have her head and they took the trakehner at a full gallop. All Georgie could do was hang on as Belle flew it easily and kept on galloping.

"Good girl!" She gave Belle a slappy pat on her sweaty neck and took hold of the reins again. The water complex was coming, but first Georgie would have to swerve to get past Kennedy who was right in their path.

This time, Kennedy couldn't fight back. Versace's stride was flagging. The horse was tired and Belle powered past him as if they were standing still.

Georgie wasn't thinking about Kennedy any more. She was utterly focused on the water complex. As Georgie took a firm grip on the reins Belle fought her, sticking her head way up in the air. They couldn't jump like this! Georgie was forced to give up the fight and let the mare do it her way. Belle flew the bank into the water and never broke out of a gallop as she churned through the pond and sprang up out the other side.

Only the coffin remained before the finish line. Belle was back in full gallop. Directly ahead of them Georgie could see the log at the top of the bank and immediately beyond it, that massive drop down the steep slope to the ditch below. Tara had made it perfectly clear. This jump needed to be taken at a canter. They had managed to make it through the water complex but there was no way they could bluff it through the coffin. If Belle came in at a gallop they would crash into the ditch.

Four strides out, Georgie knew she had two choices. She could turn the mare off now and incur a refusal and twenty faults. Or she could ride on, risking Belle's safety and her own and gallop the log fence to plunge down the bank to the ditch below.

All the way around this course she had been pretending to herself that this moment would never come. But it was unavoidable and she had to face her fear. She was only too aware that her mother had once made the wrong decision and had paid the ultimate price.

She took a deep breath. The truth was, she would never know how her mum had managed to get the jump so wrong that day. But it didn't matter. Whatever had happened, that was in the past. Georgie had to make her own choices and her own mistakes. And in that moment she knew what she had to do. She was going to jump.

Chapter Seventeen

Georgie was a brave rider, but not a foolish one. When she made up her mind to jump the coffin, she knew what she was doing.

The last time she had faced this fence she had panicked and pulled the mare off. Not this time. They were three strides out from the jump, which left her enough time to make things right. Georgie sat back heavy in the saddle and, with all her strength, gave a sharp jag on her left rein. Up until now, she had been trying to get Belle back under control by pulling on both reins. It hadn't worked because the mare had leaned against Georgie's hands and kept galloping. The sudden jerk on only one rein was enough to catch the mare in the teeth, so that she reeled back and dramatically slowed down. However, she also veered sharply to the left!

The next two strides were a blur. Georgie somehow managed to pull back on the other rein to correct Belle's line then she urged the mare on so she was once more powering ahead. Belle took the log on a perfect forward canter stride and together they flew down the slope towards the ditch below. Georgie put her legs on firmly and Belle leapt. The mare had her ears pricked forward as she cleared the ditch, then cantered back up and out over the log at the top of the bank.

The smile on Georgie's face said it all as she rode towards the finish line. She had beaten the coffin! The crowd gave her a huge cheer as she galloped on and she couldn't resist punching the air as she crossed the finish line. She hadn't won the race by any stretch – nearly half a dozen of her classmates had crossed the line well ahead of her. But she had beaten the one person that mattered. She had come home ahead of Kennedy Kirkwood.

265

All of the twelve riders had made it home safely in the end. They had spent the past hour washing down their horses, then scraping them with sweat scrapers and rugging them up before walking them for half an hour to cool down. Now the horses were all back in their fields or stalls and the young eventers were sitting nervously on hay bales at the back of the stable block, waiting for Tara Kelly to read their class rankings. She had their fates in her hands as she addressed the class.

"I'm doing this in order," Tara told them. "The best riders will be called first. When I call your name, I'll be giving your class ranking."

Georgie got the shock of her life when she heard who had crossed the line before anyone else.

"Emily Tait!" Tara Kelly said. Emily beamed with pride at her first place. There was a round of applause from the class, but Nicholas Laurent wasn't clapping. He was fuming.

"It's not fair," he complained, "she rides a Thoroughbred. Of course she will win in the steeplechase. Her horse is built to run and mine is built to jump."

266

"Oh suck it up, Laurent." Alice rolled her eyes at him.

Nicholas Laurent had taken the number two place in the class rankings. He had been followed by Cam and Daisy, who were tied for third as they had crossed the line together. Incredibly, Mitty Janssen had come fifth. She was beaming from ear to ear because her big Swedish Warmblood had jumped so well.

Georgie had risen all the way up through the numbers to come in sixth. Right behind her had been Alex Chang, who had ridden aggressively over the last three fences to take out seventh place in front of Alice in eighth. Matt Garrett had been ninth and he looked miserable about it, while Arden, in tenth, looked positively thrilled to have made it around at all.

The final two places were the ones that mattered. Because today, one of the riders in the final two would be eliminated.

"Kennedy Kirkwood," Tara Kelly said. "Will you please stand up?"

At the back of the hay bales, in the shadows, Kennedy got to her feet. As she stood up, a snigger rose from a few members of the eventing class. Kennedy, normally so glamorous and immaculate, was a mess. Her wet hair was clinging like damp rope to her sodden back protector. Her white shirt and jodhpurs were soaked through and covered in mud.

Kennedy had encountered a problem at the water jump. "She wanted to jump it one way and Versace decided to go the other!" Alice murmured to Georgie.

"Hey, Kennedy," somebody shouted out, "I love what you've done with your hair!" There was another outburst of sniggers and giggles but Tara Kelly silenced them.

"Kennedy," she said, "you were the last one across the line today, and you are to be considered for elimination." The class went quiet. "Isabel Weiss," Tara said, "would you also please stand up."

At the front of the class, Isabel stood up. She looked Tara in the eye as the instructor spoke to her.

"Isabel, you rode well today, but you retired on the course at the water complex and didn't cross the finish line." Isabel nodded. "I told you all at the start of this term that I expected to expel at least one student from my class after the mid-term exam." She looked at Kennedy and Isabel. "That student will be one of you."

The tension was unbearable. As Georgie watched the girls waiting for Tara's decision, she wanted to shout out that Kennedy deserved to go, that she had pushed her off her horse in the middle of the course. But she knew she couldn't prove it.

"Isabel," Tara said. "You are more accustomed to riding dressage than battling it out on the eventing field. Over the past four weeks however, you've proven to me that you can be a competent jumps rider. But I wonder if you have the courage that cross-country will ultimately demand of you?

"Kennedy," Tara continued. "You came into my class as the top rider from the US auditions. But being at the top means there is only one place to go. You're a born showjumper and yet from day one you have expected to naturally become the queen of the cross-country. I think today you've seen that this is not the case. Every rider needs to fight to stay at the top."

She already knows how to fight, Georgie thought. Kennedy was looking down at her feet and snivelling.

Tara paused. "Kennedy... you're still in. I'm giving you a second chance to prove yourself. I'm sorry, Isabel, but you're out."

✳

It was hard to believe that one of their classmates was gone.

"I feel so sorry for Isabel," Daisy was saying as they walked up the driveway to dinner that evening.

"Not as bad as I feel," Georgie said. "If she hadn't stopped to help me up maybe she would have tackled the water jump after all."

"It's not your fault, Georgie," Alice said and then added, "but Isabel must be devastated."

"Uhh, is that how devastated looks?" Emily asked. Ahead of them, queuing up at the door was Isabel. She was laughing and larking about as she re-enacted the elimination scene to the great delight of her dorm mates from Stars of Pau. It turned out that Isabel was neither surprised nor upset by her expulsion from Tara Kelly's class.

"I am a dressage rider," Isabel shrugged, "I never

270

wanted to be an eventer, but my instructor back home told me that I had to take Tara's class because she was the best in the business."

Half a term of eventing was more than enough for Isabel who had now swapped to a classical long-reining class.

"We're going to miss you," Georgie told her.

"Ja," Isabel shrugged, "you'll get over it. Wait 'til you see the German class rankings. I whipped all of you!"

After dinner, Georgie, Daisy, Alice, and Emily sat together in the living room at Badminton House with mugs of hot tea and chocolate biscuits recounting their rides around the point-to-point. They relived the hairy moments and shrieked with laughter at stories of near-disasters that were averted just in time.

Georgie had laughed along with them but she found it hard to join in the storytelling. It was impossible for her to describe how she had felt, especially when she had confronted the coffin.

She had asked so much of Belle and the mare had performed brilliantly. Jumping the coffin had been a rite of passage for both of them. It was almost as if they had left behind their past and formed a real bond at last. Georgie couldn't believe how lucky she was to have a horse that she adored every bit as much as Tyro.

Lucinda had been thrilled when Georgie called and told her about their point-to-point victory. She laughed when Georgie told her that instead of taking time out to celebrate, Tara had warned the class that there would be another exam at the end of the term and this time she promised it would be much tougher!

"Typical Tara!" she said. "There's never time to celebrate. She's always looking to the next fence."

"I'm so glad you've bonded with that mare," Lucinda told Georgie. "It sounds like she's a fantastic horse. And sixth in the class is a brilliant ranking to begin the year on. Your mother would be very proud."

Having used up her evening phone call quota, Georgie had emailed her exam news to her dad. Typically, he was most excited about her maths mark – she had come third in the class rankings, a fact that Dr Parker was enormously pleased about.

Are you sick of the gruel yet? Lily had written in her latest email. She was still convinced that Blainford sounded like a total nightmare. *I can't believe you've got in trouble for walking on some poxy patch of grass again!*

It had seemed like a great thing to do at the time, but now Georgie regretted storming off across the quad in front of Conrad. She had hoped Conrad might have forgotten, but then she saw the latest fatigues list had her name on it and knew she had no choice but to accept her fate and turn up at four o'clock to take her punishment.

At three fifty-five she stood by the archway next to the Great Hall with three other junior students, all of them boys from Luhmuhlen House. "I got caught talking during assembly," one boy told her.

"I didn't muck out my horse's stall," another one admitted.

The third boy, like Georgie, had mistakenly trodden on the quad. "It's just a bit of grass," he groaned. "I don't know why they make such a fuss about it."

By five minutes past four they were all getting restless. "Do you think if there's no prefect then we can just go back to the dorm?" one of the boys suggested.

"Too late," another one groaned, "here he comes."

Georgie turned to see Conrad walking along the footpath beside the quad – and James walking beside him.

"Hey, Parker," James gave her a grin.

"What are you doing here?" Georgie asked.

"I'm on fatigues," James said giving her a wink.

Conrad kept walking and the students, including James and Georgie, fell into line behind him. "Follow me," Conrad instructed. "We've got some hay bales to move down at the stables."

As they walked around the quad, Georgie tried to hang at the back of the group so that she wouldn't have to talk to James. But he slowed down intentionally, so that he could walk alongside her.

"Who gave you fatigues?" Georgie asked.

"Conrad did," James gave her a grin.

"But I thought he was your friend."

James shrugged. "Friendship with Conrad has its limits. Let's just say he got fed up with me so I'm here with you being forced into hard labour." Then he added, "I've been wanting to talk to you for weeks. You've been avoiding me ever since the polo match."

"I haven't been avoiding you," Georgie said, "I've just been making sure I'm in places where you aren't."

James laughed. "Is there something wrong with me?"

"No," Georgie said honestly. "There's something wrong with me."

She looked up into his blue eyes. "In case you haven't noticed, I'm not exactly like Arden and Tori and the showjumperettes."

"Oh, I've noticed," James grinned.

"And your sister can't stand me."

James laughed. "Parker, I wouldn't pay too much attention to my little sister. I love Kennedy, but she can be a colossal witch sometimes. And she doesn't get to choose who I can hang out with."

"What about Conrad?"

"Nah, he's not my type," James deadpanned. They were walking close and James let his hand brush against Georgie's hand. She felt her skin tingle as if an electric shock had gone through it but she pretended she hadn't noticed.

"So, you got through the first round of eventing

exams. I guess it runs in the blood," James said. "Your mum went to Blainford, didn't she?"

Georgie nodded.

"My dad came here and was this polo star," James said. "I know what it's like to have big shoes to fill."

"I used to think about that all the time," Georgie said, "but it doesn't worry me any more, at least not so much. I'm not going to compete against my mother's memory. I'm here to be the best that I can be."

James arched an eyebrow at this. "So what do you like best so far about Blainford?"

"Well, I like my new horse," Georgie said, "and my new friends..."

"...and the food in the dining hall?"

"That is most definitely not high on my list!" Georgie groaned.

"I was thinking you must be getting pretty sick of those dining hall meals by now," James said.

"Totally!" Georgie agreed. "I had a nightmare last week that involved being attacked by industrial quantities of macaroni cheese."

James laughed. "Well, that settles it then," he said.

276

"You're coming to dinner at my place."

"What?" Georgie was confused. "At Burghley House?"

"No!" James grinned. "At my house in Maryland. I'm only a weekly boarder. Mom and Dad pick me and Kennedy up and take us home most weekends – when I'm not playing polo."

Georgie noticed that James deliberately didn't mention the private jet.

"Anyway," he continued, "I can't promise anything special but Mom makes a pretty good home-cooked meal. Well, actually our chef makes it. But you get the idea."

He looked at Georgie. "So what do you say? You want to come and hang out at my place next weekend?"

When Georgie told Alice the news she shrieked so loud that she startled the horses.

"Ohmygod! James Kirkwood, *the* James Kirkwood has asked you out on a date!"

Georgie groaned, "This is exactly why I wasn't going to tell you! And, strictly speaking, he hasn't asked me out. He's asked me to go to his house."

Alice squealed even louder at this. "The Kirkwood house is, like, a total mega-mansion. It's supposed to be amazing!"

"I don't see what the big deal is," Cam huffed, as he led Paddy out of the loose box. "I mean, what does James have that I haven't got?"

"Err, do you want me to write the list or is this multiple choice?" Alice said dryly.

It was a rare occasion that the three of them had time together to go out hacking after school. It was a pity they couldn't do this every day, Georgie thought. There were so many bridle paths and the grounds were so beautiful.

The sun was low in the sky over the bluegrass pasture as they rode under a long row of white-blossomed dogwood trees. The bridle path ran alongside the novice cross-country course and Georgie could see the fences that she had jumped for the mid-term exam. None of them held any fear for her now –

but as Tara had told them, the next challenges would be far greater. As she thought about this, Georgie felt Belle snatch at the bit, wanting to canter.

Beside her, Alice was having trouble holding Will back as well. "Are you ready?" she asked Georgie and Cam. "Shall we canter?"

The three of them rose up in their stirrups and urged the horses on. Georgie looked back over her shoulder and saw the red Georgian brick buildings of the academy behind her and the horses grazing in the fields and realised for the very first time that she finally felt like she was home. She smiled at Alice and Cam and pointed at the lone dogwood in the distance. "First one to reach the tree wins," she told them.

"Come on. I'll race you."

STACY GREGG

PONY CLUB RIVALS

Showjumpers

Georgie can't wait to visit the Kirkwood mansion with James. But the showjumperettes are never far behind... Back at Blainford the rivalry hots up as Georgie and Belladonna excel in the show ring. Can they beat the showjumpers at their own game?

HarperCollins *Children's Books*

Dear Reader,

This is one of my favourite books but I still want you to take care of this book for me. I'm begging you. I don't want you to waste this book. After you've read it pass it on.

Your Sincerly,

Stacy Gregg